WRECKED

WRECKED

HEATHER HENSON

A CAITLYN DLOUHY BOOK

atheneum

NEW YORK LONDON TORONTO
SYDNEY NEW DELHI

atheneum

An imprint of Simon & Schuster Children's Publishing Division
1230 Avenue of the Americas, New York, New York 10020

For information about special discounts for bulk purchases, please contact Simon & Schuster Special Sales at 1-866-506-1949 or business@simonandschuster.com.
The Simon & Schuster Speakers Bureau can bring authors to your live event. For more information or to book an event, contact the Simon & Schuster Speakers Bureau at 1-866-248-3049 or visit our website at www.simonspeakers.com.
The text for this book was set in Dante MT Std.
Manufactured in the United States of America
First Edition
10 9 8 7 6 5 4 3 2 1
Library of Congress Cataloging-in-Publication Data
Names: Henson, Heather, author.
Title: Wrecked / Heather Henson.
Description: First edition. | New York : Atheneum Books for Young Readers, [2021] | "A Caitlyn Dlouhy book." | Audience: Ages 12 and up. | Audience: Grades 7-9. | Summary: Told from from different perspectives, almost-seventeen-year-old Miri skips school, rebuilds motorcycles, and befriends her new neighbor Fen to distract herself from knowing exactly what her dad Poe does for a living in the knobs of Kentucky.
Identifiers: LCCN 2021007360 | ISBN 9781442451056 (hardcover) | ISBN 9781442451094 (ebook)
Subjects: CYAC: Drug traffic—Fiction. | Undercover operations—Fiction. | Dating (Social customs)—Fiction. | Fathers—Fiction. | Kentucky—Fiction.
Classification: LCC PZ7.H39863 Wr 2021 | DDC [Fic]—dc23
LC record available at https://lccn.loc.gov/2021007360

FOR TIM

. . . and then, in dreaming,
The clouds methought would open and show riches
Ready to drop upon me: that when I waked
I cried to dream again.

—Caliban
From *The Tempest*
by William Shakespeare

ONE

MIRI

Poe's talking black helicopters again. Never a good sign.

"One got real close. Circled right overhead," Poe says while Miri's waiting for the coffeepot to finish doing its thing. "Can't believe you slept through it."

"I sleep the sleep of the just," Miri mumbles. Some old quote from some old book; she can't remember exactly in her precaffeinated state. Meant mostly as a joke. But Poe is serious this morning.

"You don't think I'm just?"

Miri keeps her eyes on the gurgling black liquid, stays silent. Poe's her dad—and a lot of other things besides. She does a good job of ignoring those other things. Most of the time.

"Why don't you stay home today," Poe says—not a question. He sets a plate on the island counter between them, scoots it forward.

Eggs Benedict—her favorite. Two perfect circles with disks of ham and little cloud puffs of eggs on top of English muffins, sunny yellow sauce smothering everything—hollandaise, he taught her.

Cooking used to be their thing. What they did together. In this kitchen. Not in some shack hidden way back in the woods.

"Stay home, Mir. Just for today. Just to be on the safe side." Poe's eyes are lasering in. One blue, one brown—a genetic trait Miri wished for when she was little, but is now glad she didn't inherit. Freaks most people out.

"The safe side of what?" Miri makes herself ask. "What's going on?"

Surprisingly, Poe's the first to look away.

"You know what's going on." He starts arranging the other two plates of eggs—one for himself, one for his girlfriend (and business partner), Angel. "You're not stupid," he says, and that's the last straw.

"I'm outta here," Miri says, grabbing her backpack, heading for the door.

"I've fixed you breakfast." Poe's voice is extra calm, which means a storm is coming.

"I'm not hungry," Miri tells him, a full-on lie. Her stomach's rumbling and her brain is fuzzy from lack of coffee. (Why does the machine take so long?) But she can't stay another second, can't sit at the table with Poe—and Angel when she stumbles in (she always seems hungover)—and act like nothing's weird, like they're one big happy family.

"Get back here!" The storm—with thunder and lightning—has arrived. "I've made breakfast for you, young lady, and I expect you to eat it."

"I said I'm not hungry." Slamming out the door, pounding down the porch steps.

One by one the yard dogs lift their massive heads as she passes.

Silent, all six, except for the clink of chain. They'd tear a man to shreds on Poe's command, but never so much as bare their teeth to Miri.

Is this Poe's form of being "just"? Pit bulls lined up across the yard, different intervals to confuse a possible intruder?

"To keep you safe," Poe said last year when he and Angel brought them home, "set" them up. "To keep folks out of our business."

And what business is that? Miri had wanted to ask outright, but didn't. Maybe she *is* stupid, but what choice does she have?

Poe used to fix motorcycles for a living. Not a lot of money, but enough. Especially since they have a huge garden and chickens for eggs. Especially since they hunt deer and wild turkeys, store the meat for months; go fishing whenever they want. There's always been plenty to eat. Why does Poe need more?

"Miri!" Poe's followed her out the door; he's standing on the porch. "Mir, come back, eat your food." The storm has passed—for him at least, not for her. "I'm sorry, Mir," he calls in his back-to-calm voice, but she keeps heading for the garage.

The old 1968 rebuilt Harley Sportster always takes a second kick in the morning. It balks and splutters as she dips and weaves through the deeply rutted driveway—another ploy to keep intruders out. But once she's on the paved county road, the motor stops complaining. Miri's able to open the bike all the way up, shoot like a bullet through the straightaways, lean tight and low into the twisting curves.

This is the best part of her day. Leaving Poe and Angel—leaving everything behind. Moving fast and feeling nothing. Except the wind in her face, the wind whipping through her hair. The thrum of the bike beneath her. ("The apple doesn't fall far from the tree," more than one biker's said over the years because Miri has a magic touch with fixing things, same as Poe.)

Only forty-five minutes, though—this time to herself. Forty-five minutes to pretend that she'll just keep going. Past the tiny town, past the shitty school. Out of the county, out of the state.

What would Poe do if she took off for good? Would he come after her? Would he drag her back, or let her go? She's almost seventeen but still not legal.

Poe brought Miri here when she was three years old, after her mom died. He wanted to get away from everything, start over, and he chose the hills of Kentucky, or knobs, as they're called—a kind of mini mountain, a whole ripple of mini mountains melting down toward Tennessee. He nabbed one of the topmost spots, dubbed it Paradise, and the name stuck.

Paradise Knob. Nothing official, nothing written on any map, but that's what locals call it. And Miri used to actually believe she lived in Paradise, but now she knows better.

FEN

This is not where he's supposed to be. Stranded in the middle of nowhere. A sorry-ass road in a sorry-ass state. Sorry-ass car—or truck, actually. His dad's idea.

"When in Rome," his dad had said, dropping the key to a newish / used Dodge Ram (maroon colored) into his open palm. And then promptly disappearing down his rabbit hole of a job. Like always.

"Thanks, Dad," Fen mutters now, taking yet another futile look under the jacked-open hood. Nothing seems out of place or broken; nothing screams: *Plug me in! Tighten me!*

But then, how would he know? This is the first car (truck) he's ever owned, and it's not like his dad's ever taught him anything vaguely mechanical. (His mom always calls a mechanic when she has car trouble.)

Fen would *love* to call a mechanic (do mechanics even exist in the middle of nowhere?), but he's getting zero bars on his iPhone. Same as it's been since he was transported a few days ago into this black hole of both cellular service and civilization.

"It'll be good for you," his mom kept saying once the plan to ship him off to live with his dad was set. "Get you out of Detroit for a while. Away from bad influences."

Which was insane because if his mom actually knew anything about him, anything at all, she'd understand how there were no influences—bad or good. How there were basically no real friends to lead him tragically astray. Finding his room empty a couple of times in the middle of the night didn't mean what his mom so willingly assumed.

"You, *of all people*, should know better," she kept repeating, and no matter how many times Fen tried to steer her straight, she obviously had her mind made up. "I think living with your dad is a good idea right now," she said. "I guess boys need a father figure, especially in their teen years."

"This is the perfect place to spend time together." His dad's take once the wheels were in motion. "We can do some hunting and fishing—all the stuff I used to do with my dear old dad."

Which didn't sound terrible. Fen hardly ever saw his dad anymore because he was always on the move for work. (One of the things that split his parents up in the first place, that and the drinking.) His dad's latest assignment had been in Kentucky—he'd moved down here about nine months before, had bragged over the phone to Fen about the ease of small-town Southern life.

"So . . . where's the town?" Fen had asked when his dad announced (after driving forever from the minuscule airport) that they were nearly home.

"Did you blink?" his dad joked, and it took Fen a moment to

understand that the handful of boarded-up buildings they'd just passed was it.

"Kinda remote, huh?" Fen repeated at least a couple of times as the two-lane turned to a one-lane and then—amazingly—to gravel.

"You get used to it," his dad responded, pulling up in front of a rickety old house (nothing like the bland duplexes that were his dad's usual MO). "Slower pace," he added.

"Couldn't get much slower," Fen mutters now, moving to snatch his backpack from the front seat, give the truck door a satisfying slam.

How long will it even take to walk to "town"? At least an hour, right? If not longer. Which will make him even later than he is already running for his first day of school. *First day! Woo-hoo!*

"Why can't I just finish the semester online?" he'd asked (whining a little; he just couldn't help it). But his mom had ignored the question (and the whining), had seemed intent on making him the new kid . . . yet again.

New kid . . . *walking*. And of course his trusty old Chucks aren't getting much traction on the steep incline, the slippery, faded black-top. Definitely not the best shoes for descending a mountain—or *knob*. Isn't that what his dad called it? Smaller than a mountain, bigger than a hill. So . . . knob. Dumb word. A dirty-joke kind of word.

Hey, dude, how big's your knob? (Cue to sound of snort-laughing.)

Seriously, though, the road itself is all slant. Roller-coaster verticals, which (if Fen's being honest) were making him a little buggy before his sorry-ass truck chugged to a halt for seemingly no reason.

Fen's fine with city traffic, getting on and off highways. But this corkscrew of a skinny two-lane already had him white-knuckling it most of the way.

Now Fen veers over to the nearly nonexistent shoulder, confirms it's basically a suicide drop past the (useless-looking) dented and rusted guardrails. Not much to soften your crash, big boulders and lots of trees. A river or a creek way down at the bottom. The sound of gurgling is filtering its way up through the leaves, and that's what automatically triggers a reach for the iPhone, thumb hitting record without even looking.

It's something Fen's been doing for a while now—a few years at least. Recording random stuff—ambient sound, it's called. Anything that hooks him in. And then downloading what he's captured later, onto his laptop, fooling around with it all in GarageBand, mixing it together, coming up with something new.

"Making beats" is what some people call it, but it's not that for him. It's not making music—although occasionally he does add a riff of keyboard or maybe a drumline in back—but it's more like he's creating sound. Changing it. Transforming known sound into something unknown.

Fen's read about art installations in galleries or museums that are all sound, no visuals, and he likes the idea of that, though he knows he's getting way ahead of himself there. So far, he's never even let anybody listen to his soundscapes (that's what he calls them), except for his mom and dad (separately) and they were both (separately) perplexed or even annoyed.

"Trying to write a song there, buddy?" his dad had asked. "No lyrics yet, huh?"

"Stop recording other people's conversations!" his mom had whisper-yelled after catching him a few times with the iPhone out in the produce section of Kroger or in line for a movie or something like that. "It's not nice!"

Yeah, okay, Fen sometimes records snippets of conversations, but it's not what his mom thinks. He isn't really interested in what those voices are actually saying. It's more the rhythm of the dialogue, the cadence of the words. Somebody talking—together or alone—is just another layer for his soundscapes. Like that homeless guy's looping rant that Fen happened to catch in Capitol Park at three a.m.—so perfect! A time when Fen was (totally alone) in the middle of the city, in the middle of the night, not getting drunk or high or being led astray by anything but his own need to record sounds.

Urban soundscapes are usually his thing, but maybe that's just because he's never given nature a chance, never been in the literal middle of nowhere. The stuff he's picking up now—leaves rustling, water gurgling, birds singing—it's not bad. In fact, the sound is kinda killer. Especially the birdsong—so many different birds, not just one or two. All these crazy chirps and tweets, and then this fierce high-pitched trilling that starts and stops at random. And under it all, there's a backbeat of lower notes, some short like a hammer slamming down, others stretched out, elongated, into a long, low tolling—almost like somebody's ringing a giant, ancient bell.

Fen starts zoning in on the low notes, the ancient bell bird— a little farther to the left, high up in the far-reaching boughs above his head. Unseen but heard. A distinctively deep call, steady, repetitive, predictable. Until it simply stops, and another sound vaguely takes its place. A kind of buzzing—beelike. Faint but getting louder by the second. Moving closer, dropping octaves. Shifting into a muffled rumbling, then quickly morphing into a menacing growl.

Fen's eyes pop open; he spins to face the sound. A dark shape is barreling toward him, and his brain tells him to move but his body doesn't listen.

MIRI

Luckily, she'd slowed to check out the abandoned truck—nobody she knows—a mile back, so the bike's not going full tilt when Miri comes around the bend and there's some idiot standing right in the middle of the road.

What the hell?

She swerves left, then right—not quite an overcorrect but a sharp enough swing that she has to stick one leg out and dab at the blacktop with the heel of her boot for balance. A couple more dabs, and she's back in control.

"What the *hell?*"

She checks the rearview, then swoops into a tight U so she can give the idiot a piece of her mind.

But he's already apologizing.

"Sorry!" Hands in the air, palms up. "I'm so sorry! You okay?"

Miri doesn't answer right away. She steers to the shoulder, cuts the engine but stays in a straddle just in case she has to bolt. The idiot's definitely a stranger. Dressed all in black. Tall and skinny, on the pale side. A tweaker, most likely, lost and looking for Paradise.

"What the hell?" Letting him have it for real. "You were standing right in the middle of the road. What were you thinking?"

"Yeah, that was stupid. Sorry!" He steps closer but abruptly stops when she eases the bike back a rotation. "I just . . . I guess I just spaced. I'm really, really sorry!" Taking a shaky breath. "Are you okay? I mean, shit, you almost crashed!"

Miri relaxes a bit. Guy's concern seems real enough. And now that she's gotten a solid look, he's not really fitting the tweaker profile. Skinny but not skeletal; jumpy but not twitchy. His face and arms are mostly clear—not all scratched up from "bugs" crawling everywhere. Plus, he's got a pretty impressive set of pearly whites. No rotted-out meth mouth here.

"I'm fine," she allows, though she's not ready to let the guy off the hook just yet. "But it's dangerous—wandering around in the middle of the road. Especially on these curves." She notes the black Converse high-tops and the basic backpack. "What are you doing out here anyway? Where'd you come from?"

"Detroit."

Definitely not the answer she was expecting. "Detroit." Deadpan.

"Yeah, Detroit," he repeats, raking a hand through his hair—dark and on the shaggy side. "Michigan." As if she might not know basic geography.

"And . . . let me guess . . ." Cocking her head. "You're lost."

"Yeah. You could say I'm lost." The slow, sideways grin takes her by surprise, throws her a little off balance.

"Where you trying to go?" she asks, glancing away, avoiding the urge to grin back.

"Actually, it's my first day of school," he says, and before she can call him on it, explain how she knows all the kids—buzzards, she's dubbed them—at the one and only high school in these parts, he's giving her the whole story. "I just moved here to live with my dad, and yeah, the semester's almost over, but my mom insisted. And my truck broke down and I'm not getting any service at all." Pulling a cell phone out of his back pocket, waving it in the air. "Do you get any service up here?"

"Not really," she says. Easier than explaining how she doesn't own a cell phone, never has. "So that's your truck back there?" Pieces of a puzzle fitting together inside her head. "What's wrong with it? Battery die or something?"

"Maybe?" Still focused on the phone, holding it at different angles. "It just kinda . . . stopped? I'm not very good with things like that."

Miri shifts the weight of the bike, centers it. "I could run back up and take a look if you want."

"Take a look?" Totally confused.

"Yeah, I'm pretty good with things like that." Not bragging, just stating a fact. And it's so typical—the *Huh? Girls can fix cars?* look that always comes next.

"Okay . . . if you think . . . ," he begins, but Miri kick-starts the engine, lets the roar drown out the rest of his words.

"See you up there," she yells over her shoulder as she glides past, leaning her weight into the turn, gearing back up the road.

The truck's actually pretty sweet, she decides, after she's parked, given it a once-over. Not brand-new, but nearly. No dents or patched-up rust she can see. Clear coat buffed to a glossy shine. A Dodge Ram doesn't exactly match this guy, Detroit's, vibe—the black jeans and black T-shirt, black high-tops. But maybe it's a city-boy-trying-out-a-country-boy thing.

"Your cables are tight and there's no corrosion around the battery," she tells him when he appears.

"Okay . . . ?" Huffing a little from the straight uphill jog—probably not a jock.

"Had it awhile?" Miri reaches for the dipstick. Surely, Detroit checked the oil, but then again, maybe not.

"No, I just got it."

Oil level's fine; water tank's full. Hoses seem to be connected to all the right places. "Off the lot or sale-by-owner?" she asks.

"Um, not exactly sure?"

Miri eases herself out from under the hood. "You're not exactly sure where you got *your* truck?"

"Not really . . . ?"

She takes a step back. Maybe she's misread the situation; maybe this is some kind of con or scam.

"My dad got it for me. Thought I needed a truck around here. Had some dude bring it to our house."

Quickly Miri scans the woods, checking for somebody hiding behind a tree, a partner maybe. "So . . . this is your truck," she says, leveling her gaze, locking eyes. "And the motor just . . . died." Liars will get squirrely, shift where they look—something Poe's taught her.

"Yeah, like I said, it just seemed to, like, stop for no reason." His eyes—a deep brown—stay locked. "I've actually never driven it before today." Deer eyes—that's what they remind her of. Dark and wide and trusting; prey, not predator. "Never even driven a truck, if you want to know the truth. It was just my mom's old beat-up Honda Civic back home."

Miri watches him a moment longer, then leans back under the hood without comment. She checks the oil a second time, just to be sure, swiping her greasy fingers against her back pockets—one more stain to add to the collection. *My little grease monkey*—what Poe used to call her.

"Mind if I try to start 'er up?" Miri heads around to the driver's side without waiting for an answer. "I'll get a better idea if I can hear what's going on."

"Sure." Detroit follows, fishing into his jeans pocket for the key.

Inside the cab, Miri breathes in the new-car smell, eyes the gunkless cup holders. When she turns the key, the motor wants to crank, which means it's not the battery. Maybe the alternator, or the starter? She tries again and it's odd because she can hear how the engine is making an effort to catch, turn over. But something's stopping it, something's not quite . . .

"Gas," she mumbles, feeling like an idiot herself. *Always check your gas before you head out*, she can practically hear Poe say. "You're out of gas," she clarifies because Detroit's face has gone blank.

"But . . ." Disbelieving. "Isn't there, like, a warning light or something?"

"Yeah, it comes on when you turn the key." Tapping the little plastic window, the perky spot of orange. "You must not've noticed."

"No way." Detroit has moved in for a closer look, and Miri gets a whiff of soap and laundry detergent—guy's super clean. Cheeks totally smooth, shaved. No scraggly patches, the wannabe-beard most dudes at school start sporting the moment they can.

"Stupid," Detroit says under his breath. "Really stupid." His skin's pale, but that's changing fast—a blotch of pink, and then another—cabbage roses blooming along his neck. Miri has a sudden crazy urge to put her fingers to his throat, feel the heat he must be radiating.

"You have an extra tank in the back, right?" she says, sliding past Detroit. She checks the truck bed—empty, clean as a whistle. "Um, maybe you have some gas back at your house?" But even as it's out, she knows it's doubtful, given this guy's track record so far. "Where do you live anyway?" Realizing it must be close since he stalled this far up the knob. "The old Gooch place?"

"I think so? Maybe? My dad's been there about nine months or so."

Okay, how'd she miss *that*? A new neighbor? And how'd Poe not know about it either?

"Can't believe my dad gave me a truck on empty!" Detroit mutters, hand raking hair again. "Great! Thanks, Dad!"

"Maybe he didn't know," Miri offers. "You said somebody delivered it to your house. Maybe the guy stiffed your dad."

"Why would he do that?" Curious.

Because you're not from around here, which makes you an easy mark. What she could say, but doesn't. "Gas is high." She shrugs. "Guy was probably just trying to save a few bucks."

Detroit nods, accepting that. He pockets the phone without checking it again. "How close is the nearest station?"

"Not close. But that's okay." She turns toward her bike. "We've got some extra gas at our place. I'll just run and grab a two-gallon tank. That'll be enough to get you to school. And then to the BP sta-tion afterward," she adds. "Get yourself an extra tank while you're there. Good to have a gallon or two around. Long way between fill-ups here."

"That's a lot of trouble for you." Detroit is following close behind. "And I'm making you late for school. You're headed there too, right?"

Miri grabs the handlebar, swings her leg over the saddle. "Don't worry about it." She takes a breath—should she be honest? "Hate to spoil your first day. But school here's basically a shit hole."

He gives a laugh—short, sharp. "Not really surprised. Not my first shit hole."

Miri resists the urge to follow up on that. She wasn't raised nosy—not with Poe for a dad.

"I could come with you," Detroit offers. "Help you carry the tank."

Miri's about to say no. Not a lot of room on the back of the bike, and besides, she's hauled plenty of gas—you just strap the tank to the tail rack with a couple of bungees.

"I'm Fen, by the way." Sticking out a hand—old-school. *"Fen, not Finn,"* he clarifies. "Fen's short for Fenton—a family name. Fen Kingston."

"Miri." Taking the hand, giving it a shake. *"Miri, not Mary."* Because people get her name wrong all the time.

"So . . . I guess we're kinda the same," he says, and there's that sideways grin again. "Our names. They're both a little . . . tricky."

"Yeah." Feeling her own lips tugging up, no way to resist this time. "I guess you're right." And before she knows what she's doing, she's already asking, "Ever ridden on the back of a bike before?"

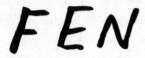

FEN

It's awkward, he has to admit. Wrapping yourself around somebody—a girl—you've just met.

"Hold on tight!" Miri's called over her shoulder a couple of times when he's tried to (politely) loosen his grip. "Or you're going to slide right off!"

So, he's doing just that. Holding Miri tight around the waist, tucking himself close as he can—not a whole lot of room on the seat. He hadn't really thought that one through when he offered to help with the gas tank. He hadn't thought about helmets, either.

"Rider's choice. Not state law," she'd told him once he finally asked, *after* they were already in motion, zipping along the roller-coaster road. "But don't worry, I'll take it slow." A pause. "And hopefully there won't be some idiot standing in the middle of the road at the next turn."

He'd laughed out loud at that—good one.

"It's an old bike," she explains when the motor stutters and

seems to balk on a particularly steep stretch. He's about to offer
to get off and push, but she does some quick shifting, some fierce
revving, and then they're up and over, the ride smoothing out. "I
rebuilt it myself from a vintage Harley, a 1968 Sportster."

"Cool." He doesn't know anything about motorcycles—*bikes*.
But Harley's badass, no question. "Cool."

As they come to his driveway, he points it out—relieved no one
can see the house from the road. "Like I said, my dad moved here
first, like almost a year ago, but I just made it the other day."

"Your dad fix it up?" Miri asks like she's read his mind. "The
house's been empty awhile."

"Doesn't seem like it," he admits. "Pretty rough." He waits for
her to ask more questions—like what his dad does that brought
him here—but she doesn't. She just keeps looping them skyward.
He can't believe somebody lives farther up the mountain—knob—
than he does. He closes his eyes and lets the sound take over.
The rush of wind combined with the low growl of the bike's motor.
He wants to reach into his pocket, grab his phone, capture it. But
he'd probably drop it, and that would suck.

When Fen opens his eyes again, the trees are still speeding past—
extra-fast motion. He tries to focus his gaze on just one trunk as
they go, but it's impossible. So he lets his eyes unfocus—a blur of
green, obscured occasionally by the tangle of Miri's hair, coppery
colored, tickling at his face, giving off a faint scent of flowers mixed
in with something sharp, metallic.

"Here we are!" Miri's voice breaks into his lulled-out daze.
"Hold on," she warns again, even though he hasn't relaxed his grip
at all.

As soon as they're off the main road, he gets it. The driveway—if that's what you want to call it—is crazy, more like a bombed-out war zone. No gravel, like at his place. Just packed earth blasted through with giant holes—craters—and Miri has to keep slowing to slalom around or through them. Fen keeps bumping up against her, he can't help it. Which is making things awkward all over again, at least for him. He keeps watching for a house, but it's all just trees and more trees. Does everybody around here live as far back in the woods as they can possibly get?

Miri brings the bike to a sudden halt, which makes Fen slam into her for about the fiftieth time. "Hey, mind waiting here?"

"Sorry!" he blurts, scooting back.

"It's okay," Miri says. "But it might be better if I go on ahead and get the tank. I won't be a minute."

"Sure!" Fen remembers to swing his leg wide as he's getting off—to avoid the burning-hot exhaust pipe, something she'd warned him about from the first. "No problem."

"Sorry," she says, and he's not sure why *she's* apologizing. *He's* the one practically squeezing her to death, jolting into her every second. "It's just . . ." She's got her head down, tangly hair hiding her face. "Poe can be funny about strangers. I'll just run to the garage and be back in a sec."

"Sure," Fen repeats. "I'm good here."

"Great." Her head comes up, and he catches a look in her eyes—fear, anger, sadness—hard to tell which.

"Who's Poe?" he decides to ask.

"My dad." Her eyes shoot forward, and then she's revving the engine, taking off down the war-zone driveway.

MIRI

She lost her nerve at the last minute—couldn't bring Fen all the way to the garage. What if Poe and Angel are still eating breakfast? What if Poe hears the bike and comes down to apologize for wigging out earlier? One look at Fen and the storm would blow up all over again.

Miri knows Fen must think she's weird—ditching him in the middle of the driveway. But what else could she do? It's not like she's ever brought anyone home before. It's not like she has any friends. Except Clay, of course. And she's not even sure about that—at least not lately.

Miri slaloms around the potholes and ruts per usual—quick as she can. When she's up and over the ridge, gravel beneath her wheels, her focus goes to the front wall of windows. She keeps watching, but there's no movement, no sign of life. The yard dogs do rattle their chains a bit, shifting positions, but they know the sound of her bike, her scent even, so they don't make a peep.

Quickly she grabs one of the extra gas tanks from the corner of the garage, attaches it with a bungee to the tail bar like she'd originally planned. Relief floods through her as she heads back to get Fen. She'll take him to his truck, she'll get him gassed up and on his way to school. Maybe she'll follow or maybe she'll just skip like Poe wanted her to in the first place. The thought of arriving this late with a new kid makes her stomach clench. She hates to give the buzzards something to pick over.

But, coming around the bend, her bike nearly goes into the second skid of the day. *What the hell?* Fen's right where she left him, but the problem is, he's not alone.

"Shit!" She guns her motor, nearly wheelies forward. Because Clay's there too. And he's got one of Poe's rifles—the AR-556, she'd know it at any distance—and he's pointing it right at Fen.

CLAY

This was his mom's place before Poe took over, and so maybe it should be Clay's by rights, the whole thing, not just the patch of land the trailer's on, but Poe's always been good to Clay. Raised him almost like his own son, gave him work once he quit school.

Odd jobs, that's what Clay mainly does for Poe. Pickups, deliveries. In the old days Clay might've been a smurf like his mom. Cora used to drag him from town to town, leave him buckled in his car seat while she'd hit every Walmart or Dollar Store or CVS or Rite Aid in a hundred-mile radius. Buy up all the boxes of Sudafed she could, turn around, try it again two days later. Different stores—big ones, but also the mom-and-pop places that were still hanging on somehow in half-empty towns.

"We're smurfs," she'd tell him, referring to some old cartoon he'd never even seen. "I'm mama smurf and you're my baby smurf," she'd say, making her voice go funny, making him laugh though he didn't totally understand until much later.

Smurfs—an old TV cartoon, yeah, but also a nickname for people like his mom—methheads—going from town to town, buying up, "smurfing" all the cold medicine they could find.

"Shush now, baby smurf," she'd whisper when she'd tuck a box of Sudafed beneath his bottom while he was sitting in the grocery cart—too old, too big, but wedged in anyway—stick another box between his back and the metal frame. Sometimes the alarm would go off as they were rolling out of the store, but she'd make a scene, yank her receipt out of her bag, hold it up high.

"There's nothing in here I didn't pay for! You can check it all yourself, but hurry because I gotta get my kid outside. I think he's gonna puke."

And Clay knew that was his cue to put a hand to his belly, start moaning. And the register guy, or the manager, if it'd gone that far, would wave his arms in the air, shooing them out.

"Go on, miss, it's fine. Probably just a glitch with the scanner."

Maybe things would've been okay if Cora had just stuck to smurfing, but she started cooking, too. Crystal Cora. That's what everybody around here started calling her. She was a big deal for a while. But then things went to shit because she was high all the time. And then Cora's place got raided and the judge gave her twenty years up at KCIW, and they lost their land. That's when Poe came along, and from the get-go he treated Clay like family when he didn't have to.

Lately Poe has been asking him to walk around the place, act like security, which is fine, Clay can do that. He chose the Ruger this morning—not Poe's fanciest AR-15 but one Clay is partial to—the weight of it slung over his shoulder, solid and comforting. Though it's not like he's really expecting any trouble. Poe's probably going paranoid, same as Cora, same as everybody gets, working around crank.

But then he hears a motor rumbling. He goes perfectly still to listen—Miri. Coming back from school way too early. Maybe she forgot something; maybe she decided to skip. Now might be a good time to apologize for the other day.

Clay comes out of the woods and starts down the driveway toward the garage. But then he sees some guy—a complete stranger—standing right in the middle of the road, and his heart thumps into overtime.

"Hands up!" Clay shouts, swinging the Ruger into place. "Hands up where I can see them."

Instantly, the guy obeys and whirls around—a deer-in-the-headlights look on his face, and not even a buck or a mama deer, but a baby, a fawn.

Clay is just about to lower the rifle because, honestly, this kid—definitely a kid, a year or two younger at least—this Bambi, seems pretty harmless.

But then Miri's bike is roaring back down the drive. And Miri herself is cutting the engine, flying at him, eyes flashing.

"Clay! What the hell?"

FEN

It's nothing like on TV or in the movies or playing a round of *Call of Duty*. Some big, beefy dude dressed all in camo, standing not ten feet away, aiming a semiautomatic straight at your chest.

Fen's guts turn liquid and his knees go weak. He's sure he's going to shit himself or sink to the ground, or both at once.

But then he hears a familiar growl, and before he knows what's happening, Miri's back, and she's off the bike and rushing the camo dude, getting right in his face. Which is crazy! Does she not see the gun?

"What the hell?" Same phrase she used to greet Fen. "What the hell's going on?"

"Who the hell's this guy?" camo dude lobs back, but he's already lowering the rifle, slinging it by its strap over his (broad) shoulder. And then the two of them are hunched together—the guy towering over Miri—talking in hushed voices.

"So . . . Fen." Miri finally turns his way. "This is Clay. He's . . . my neighbor." Shooting an arm out between them. "Clay . . . this is Fen. He's new around here."

Fen doesn't move, doesn't make a sound, and neither does "Clay." Not at first. But then the guy reaches up, adjusting the bill of his camo cap, scratching at his blondish beard. "Hey," he says, so Fen goes ahead and says "Hey" back.

And that's it for what seems like a lifetime. But then Miri jumps in. "Clay lives on the knob, he grew up here. He has a trailer not that far from here. And he works for Poe, my dad . . . does odd jobs." Miri seems to be rambling. "He helps out. And sometimes he does a little . . . hunting."

"What're you hunting now?" Fen blurts—he can't help it. He might be a city boy, but he's not a complete idiot. He knows most hunting happens in the fall.

"Anything that moves."

Seriously?

Miri lets out a laugh—big, loud. Fake. "Groundhogs, mostly! Groundhogs are cute, but there're too many this time of year. They tunnel through everything, destroy the garden if you don't watch out." She gestures out like the driveway is suddenly riddled with furry little bodies. "Clay was hunting . . . groundhogs."

"Cool," Fen says, nodding. "Cool," he repeats even though he's not buying any of it. He's not sure why Miri's covering for this guy, but he knows a semiautomatic when he sees one. Definitely more firepower than you need for going after *groundhogs*.

"Clay's family used to own all this land," Miri is saying. "But then Poe bought it when we moved here, when I was, like, three.

And then Clay stayed on after his mom—" Miri stops. "After his mom . . ." Her words trail off.

"Sorry," Fen offers, assuming Clay's mom died or something. "I'm sorry," he repeats, truly meaning it, but when he glances over, Clay's staring at him like he's literally covered in shit.

"Sorry my mom's in prison?" Clay gives a snort, then leans to one side and spits—actually spits—something dark and wet that makes a heavy splatting sound in the dirt near his own big black boot. "Later, Mir," he mumbles, turning away, heading for the woods, melting soundlessly—despite his size—into the trees.

MIRI

It's because he tried to kiss her and she laughed—that's why Clay's been acting weird.

The thing is, she couldn't help it; she thought it was a joke at first.

"I'm sorry!" she'd cried when she realized Clay was serious. "I'm sorry!" she'd repeated after he'd jumped up from where they'd been sitting side by side, working together on the new (old) Panhead she's rebuilding. "Come back!"

But Clay didn't come back. He just stalked out the garage door, down the driveway toward his trailer. And he didn't show up for dinner that night like usual. And he didn't show up at the garage the next day after she got home from school, or the next, either.

In fact, Miri hadn't seen Clay for over a week—until today—a record breaker, when she stops to think about it. Clay's always been around, pretty much for as long as Miri can remember.

Whenever Poe was too busy, it was Clay who'd look after her, even though he was only three years older. They'd roam in the woods; he'd show her cool things like blue salamanders hiding under rocks, garden spiders writing messages in their webs, Jesus bugs walking across creek water. A baby owl once that had fallen from its nest—something so soft and light inside her cupped hands she could hardly feel it. She and Clay had nursed the baby back to health and let it go free once it could fly. She thinks she still hears it sometimes, sees it, flying overhead. A good-luck charm.

A big brother, that's how she thinks of Clay. So the kiss—it caught her off guard. But she shouldn't have laughed—how could she be so dense? Clay obviously thought she was laughing *at* him. Just like the buzzards at school, those assholes who used to make fun of him before he dropped out for good. They'd tease Clay for being slow. But he's not slow, not at all—just smart in a way that isn't obvious at first.

Clay does odd jobs around Paradise for Poe, but after Miri's home from school, he usually hangs out, helping her tinker with bikes. Most of the time they just talk about random stuff, or nothing at all, it doesn't matter. But that day Miri remembers they were talking about where they'd want to go if they actually ever left the knobs—which is something Miri has been obsessing about lately.

"The desert," Miri said. "Definitely the desert."

"Why?" Clay asked.

"Because the desert doesn't have any trees," she answered. "I'm sick of all these frickin' trees." Not really true, but for some reason it felt good to say. "I want to be able to see a whole sky of stars— like miles and miles—not just a patch here and there."

"You could take me with you."

"And I want to try to race on sand. I've been reading about these old sand-dragger bikes people used to build in the sixties. They used to race them across the desert in the middle of the night."

"You could take me with you."

She'd heard him the first time, but she was on a roll.

"Tiny headlamps and they'd be dodging cacti and boulders and these abandoned mine shafts, so it was touch and go about whether you'd even survive the race."

"I want to go with you." The words were different, and they were louder this time. And then Clay had leaned in close and put his mouth onto hers.

It's not that it felt bad. More that it was odd, funny—ticklish with Clay's beard, a joke maybe. A way to get her to stop rambling on like she knows she does sometimes. So she started laughing, she couldn't help it.

And that's when Clay jumped up, rushed off. But not before Miri caught the look in his eyes. Like an animal that's been wounded. She'd seen Clay look that way before. But never because of something *she'd* done.

FEN

"What's his mom in prison for?" Fen decides to go ahead and ask Miri. Once they've shot back down the mountain (knob) with the bright-red plastic tank wedged awkwardly to one side; once they've emptied the gas into the truck.

"The usual around here." Miri doesn't look up, busy strapping the tank back onto her motorcycle. "Meth."

"Okay." Not sure what else to say. He'd been wondering why his dad ended up here—so far from a city or even a town. Hasn't had a chance to ask. "So . . . I guess it's bad here? Drugs . . . meth?"

"You could say that." Tugging on the bungee cord, testing it.

Fen wants to ask about the gun—maybe Miri'd come clean about why camo dude Clay was carrying it, now that they're alone.

"You're all set," she says, and the moment passes. "Like I said, you should get your own tank when you're at the BP, keep it for emergencies."

"Thanks." Fen reaches into his back pocket. "Hey, how much do I owe you?"

"Forget about it." She waves the wallet away, gets back on the bike. "That's what neighbors are for, I guess."

"Yeah, I guess so."

Fen watches her roll off the kickstand, straighten the front tire. Time to go—he knows it, but he can't seem to move. He's not thrilled about school, especially now that he knows it's a "shit hole," but it's more than that. He doesn't want to leave Miri—which is stupid because, first of all, they've just met, and second of all, they're headed to the exact same place. But he knows how things go. People usually act different in school. Lots of times they don't mean to, but that's just the way it is.

"Guess I'll see you down there, then." Reaching deep into his pocket for the key. "Better late than never, right?" Is it obvious he's stalling?

"You go on ahead." There's a longish pause. "I think I'm going to skip today." She's got her head down again, fooling with some cables, so he can't see her face.

"You feeling sick or something?" He takes a step closer. "I could help. Run and get you—" Stopping short. No drugstores around here—*duh!*

"Nah, I'm fine," she says. "It's just . . ." Words trailing off.

"School's a shit hole?"

Miri has a tiny gap between her two front teeth—visible when she smiles full-out, but this time her lips stay pressed together.

"Not just that."

"Won't you get into trouble?" His thoughts jump back to the

war-zone driveway, what she said about her dad—how he didn't like strangers. "Wouldn't your dad—Poe—be pissed?"

"Nah, not really." She's back to fiddling with the cables. "It's complicated."

"Can I do anything? Help somehow?" Stupid question—what's *he* going to do exactly? He's the new kid around here, and besides, she's the one who basically came to his rescue with the gas. "I could skip with you." He says it before he can change his mind, wimp out. Crazy idea, totally crazy, and yet . . .

"But it's your first day . . ." Not sounding totally horrified by the suggestion.

"It doesn't have to be!" Some kind of force is taking over. "I could just . . . tell school the move took longer than we thought, and I got here a day late."

"But what about *your* dad? Won't he be pissed?"

"He'll never even know." Wondering as he says it if it's really true. "My dad gets totally wrapped up in his work." Definitely true. "And besides, school'll never even get through to him." Pulling out the useless phone. "I know he's not getting any service. We've got the same sucky plan."

"If you're sure . . ." She's studying him now, eyes narrowed. Not so different from how camo dude Clay was staring at him, like Fen's a target. But this time he doesn't mind.

"Yeah, I'm sure," he says. For a quick moment, he thinks about his mom, how she believed the country would be better for him right now, and yeah, Fen has to admit, it already is—but probably not for the reasons she imagined.

MIRI

The old Gooch place is a little less ramshackle than it used to be. The busted-in porch has been leveled, the shot-out windows replaced, a new coat of gray paint slapped over everything. Still, it's not super inviting. Miri wonders what brought Fen's dad here, but of course she's not going to ask.

"Home sweet home," Fen says—loaded with obvious irony. "Want to come inside, take the grand tour?"

"Maybe we could just hang out here?" It's not that she doesn't trust Fen, it's just . . . it's probably weird to go into somebody's house after you've just met. Of course, it's probably even weirder to *skip school* with somebody you've just met. Somehow Fen doesn't feel like a stranger exactly, though he doesn't feel totally familiar, either.

"There's a creek down the hill, behind your house," Miri offers. "Pretty sweet. Seen it yet?"

He shakes his head. "Haven't done much exploring. Was mainly unpacking boxes all weekend."

"C'mon, I'll show it to you." Miri goes to grab her water bottle, the one she keeps strapped to her bike, and then they set off. "Just gotta find the right deer path," she mutters, more to herself. It's been a while since she's hiked to the creek from this side of the knob. "Should be over here . . ." Leading the way, waiting for Fen to catch up before ducking into the woods ahead of him.

"This is probably a stupid question," Fen says after they've made a few downward spirals through the scrubby trees and rock ledges. "But if it's a 'deer path,' does that mean that deer made it?"

"Yep," Miri answers. "Over time, and lots and lots of deer. That's actually why the roads around here are so windy. When settlers came, they'd just start expanding the paths into roads, but they wouldn't bother straightening them out too much."

"Yeah, that main road?" Fen snorts. "More like a roller coaster."

Miri laughs. "You get used to it."

They keep going, and the path turns "roller coaster" just like the main road. Fen keeps slipping—sneakers must have no traction. She glances back a couple of times to make sure he's okay, and he's always got his phone out.

"If you weren't getting service on the road," Miri points out, "you're definitely not gonna get anything down here."

"No, it's . . ." He shakes his head, and it seems like he's about to say something but stops. "Yeah, zero bars."

They continue on downhill in silence—well, not total silence. The twigs are snapping under their feet. ("Too loud!" Clay would scold if he were here.) And the squirrels and chipmunks are rustling everywhere. The birds are squawking—especially the blue jays staking out their claims, fighting over their territory.

"What kind of bird is that?" Fen asks.

"The annoying one?"

"Yeah." He chuckles. "The annoying one."

"Couple of blue jays duking it out."

"Like fighting?"

"Yeah. Lots of birds will get all protective over their space, but blue jays are extra loud about it. Tough birds. Not so nice."

"Angry birds." Fen chuckles again.

Miri doesn't respond. She gets the basic reference, though she's always kind of out of it when it comes to stuff most kids know about. "Blue jays are always picking fights," she explains. "They'll even steal nests from other birds, roll the eggs out and smash them."

"So, basically, they're the assholes of the bird world."

Grinning. "Basically."

"Are there any bears around here?" Fen asks when they take a break and she offers him some of her water. "I mean, do we need to be worried? In Montana—I lived there for a little while—you had to always be really careful about bears, like you couldn't leave your garbage out or anything."

"There used to be bears—black bears—but that was a long time ago," she assures him. "All gone now. I mean, every once in a while somebody'll claim they've seen one, but Clay's never found any signs. And he's really good at tracking things."

"Like groundhogs?"

That nearly makes her spit out her water. "Yeah, like groundhogs." Avoiding Fen's eye as she recaps the bottle. Does he suspect something was off back there with Clay? Well, he's right. Something *is* off.

As soon as she gets back home, she needs to talk to Clay. Poe's obviously going off some kind of deep end lately—black helicopters and all that—but Clay doesn't have to follow. Clay's nineteen. He doesn't have to stick around here and go down the same path his mom did. He should take off while he can—not wait for Miri like he talked about doing.

"Creek's not much farther," she says, getting them moving again. "We're coming to the bottomland soon."

"Bottomland?"

"Where everything flattens out."

"Flat would be good. Have to admit my Chucks aren't exactly cutting it here. I'll probably need to invest in some boots."

"Not a bad idea," Miri agrees.

"Yours are awesome."

Miri glances down at her scuffed toes. "They're old, but they work."

"Definitely kick-ass."

"Thanks." Miri shrugs like it's no big deal, but inwardly she's smiling. Angel calls her "hopeless" when it comes to fashion. She's always buying Miri tiny skirts and tank tops—high heels even. What's the point of high heels anyway? You can't ride in them, can't walk for shit in them.

The slant is leveling out and the trees are starting to thin; the ground turning a vibrant green—lush grass rolling gently to the creek.

"I'm guessing this is the bottomland," Fen observes, and Miri nods. He stops and closes his eyes. "I like the sound." Pausing. "I guess brooks really do babble—something you hear in books."

"Creeks definitely talk," Miri agrees, heading over to the rock ledge she and Clay sit on when they come this way to hunt in the fall—deer, not groundhogs. "This is a good place to hang out," she says when Fen catches up. "Good place to dip your toes." Plopping down and immediately starting to work on her laces.

"Yeah, it's kinda sticky," Fen says, plucking at his T-shirt—damp in places where the sweat's come through. "Is it always this hot?"

"You ain't seen nothing yet." She offers him the water bottle again, and he takes a swig before tackling his own shoes—Chucks, he called them, another name for Converse, Miri's guessing.

"Is there a pool to go to around here in the summer?"

"There's a swimming hole."

"A swimming *hole*?" Shooting her an *Are you serious?* look. "Like a pond or something?"

Miri finishes rolling up her jeans, and eases both feet into the water—ice-cold, but she decides not to mention that, not to react at all. "Yeah, a pond. A big one," she answers finally. The cold is excruciating, but at the same time, delicious. "And we go to Hidden Waterfall sometimes. Good place to swim."

"You and your friends?" he asks, and she nods—better than explaining how she doesn't really have any friends, except Clay.

Fen releases one foot from its high-top and then the other, tugs off his black socks. His feet are long and thin—delicate. Miri's seen guys' feet before (Clay's are huge; Poe's are gnarly), but Fen's are graceful, almost beautiful. She glances away, flushing. Because it's like she's just seen Fen naked or something.

"How do you hide a waterfall anyway?" Fen is asking.

"That's just what it's called," she answers. "Hidden Waterfall. A place only the locals go."

"I guess I'm a local now," he says, sounding so sure of himself, but then he sticks those graceful, beautiful feet in the water and instantly he's yelping and jerking them out again.

"It's freezing!" he cries. "It's fucking freezing!" He turns to her, totally shocked but laughing. "Why didn't you tell me?"

"Sorry . . . ?" Trying to keep a straight face.

"Thanks a lot." He rolls his eyes, still laughing. "No way I'm putting my feet back in there. No way."

"Guess you're not a local, then." Shrugging, paddling her own feet nonchalantly back and forth in the (now) refreshing cold. "'Cause locals are tough."

"Oh yeah?" Going serious now. "Watch this." Plunging both feet into the water, wincing but not making a peep.

CLAY

"Care for a beer, son?"

Clay nods, holds a hand out. He likes when Poe calls him son. Likes when he hands him an icy brown bottle over the counter and clinks it with his own—man to man, equals.

Clay puts the beer to his lips and takes a hard pull and it's good because it's so cold and today's been hot, hotter than usual.

"Thanks," he says before the second pull.

"You're welcome, son."

And for a moment while they're silent, standing together, drinking their beer, Clay imagines—not for the first time—what it would be like to actually be Poe's son, to live in this house Poe built with his own two hands, to really be a part of Poe's vast operation, not just a small piece. To be respected like Poe is, not ridden for having a methhead mom in prison, a dad not even Cora knew for sure.

"Could've been anybody," Cora said the last time he visited her in prison. "I won't lie. Your daddy could've been anybody. Back then. It wasn't my best time."

"When was your best time, Cora?"

Something he didn't ask then. Only after he'd gotten back home, back to the trailer. A few beers secretly snagged from Poe's stash, talking to the photo that was still taped to the fridge. Cora when she was about his age.

"The time you left me locked in the car in the cold while you went to score? Or maybe that time you tried to feed me dog food because you got the cans confused?"

But he'd stopped then. He was tipsy and he was talking to himself. And besides, it hadn't been bad every single minute.

There was the time Cora brought home about twenty gallons of ice cream from the Dollar Store where she worked for a while because the freezers had all gone out, so they ate only ice cream morning, noon, and night. Or the time she just suddenly swerved off the exit on I-65 and took him to Kentucky Down Under so they could see a real kangaroo.

"Anything happen today, son?"

Poe's voice snaps Clay out of the Cora whirlpool, something he gets sucked into more and more as he gets older and realizes what a truly terrible childhood he had. Maybe he should just stop visiting her; it never does him any good. She's not getting out anytime soon, either. Keeps getting in trouble.

"No, sir," Clay answers automatically even though his thoughts are sliding to that guy. Fen—what kind of name is that? And what's his deal anyway? Dressed all in black, standing in the middle of the road, obviously scared shitless like some Bambi. "Nothing," he adds, and he doesn't feel *too* guilty about lying, because the lie has to do with Miri. He's not thrilled by the fact that the lie has to do with Miri—why did she bring Fen here anyway? But he'll cover for Miri because, well, he loves her. There. He said (thought) it. He didn't know before. Or maybe he didn't know it in the same way. But he does now.

"Nothing suspicious," he says, loudly and firmly, because Poe's doing that thing where it's like he's looking directly into your brain, reading your mind.

It has to do with his eyes—the two different colors. Clay thought Poe was a demon when he first saw him. Cora always talked about ghosts and demons living in the woods—whether she was high off her ass or not.

"Some people say your great-great-granddaddy was a demon living in these woods," she'd say, "and that's why your great-great-granny couldn't leave this place, why none of us can leave this place."

You left this place.

Clay thinks it, but of course doesn't say it because he's having a conversation in real time with Poe.

"Glad to hear it. Didn't really expect anything," Poe says. "But you can never be too careful."

"No, sir, you can never be too careful." Clay takes another swig to clear his thoughts—not that beer is exactly right for the job. But just holding the cold bottle, concentrating on the cold liquid inside his mouth moving down his throat, does help focus things. Sometimes there's so much in his head, so many conversations, he gets all tangled up.

That's why he dropped out of school. Because he couldn't keep his thoughts focused, plus, nobody really expected him to finish anyway. Not even Poe and Miri, who'd always been on his side, always told him he's smarter than he thinks.

"Wouldn't mind you taking a night shift too," Poe says. "Maybe about midnight. Something keeps waking me up."

"Yes, sir." Clay finishes off the last of the beer and sets it in the recycle bin. He'd never heard of recycling before Poe showed up. And he still doesn't totally get it. Most people around here throw their empties in a pile right outside their kitchen door, or maybe they take them a little farther into the woods. But Poe actually has him take this whole big bin down the hill, to the county Dumpster on the other side of town.

"And as always, you're welcome to stay for dinner, son. I'm trying out some pork chops topped in a balsamic cherry sauce."

"Okay, thanks." Clay loves eating here, loves Poe's cooking. A little funny that Poe is a good cook all the way around—in the kitchen and in the lab. Not that Clay's tasted any crystal. Never been tempted there. Not with a mom like Cora. But he's heard the talk.

"Clear as ice."

"Smooth."

Poe is good at what he does. And he's good at keeping it all separate. Miri, his own daughter, isn't involved, didn't understand what was going on until Clay himself started to let it slip.

Never eat what you cook.

Poe's number one rule, written in stone. Everybody who works for Poe has to abide by it. Or they're gone. Cora never would've made it. Lately, Clay wonders if Angel will last much longer—she's definitely starting to look and act like a tweaker.

"Hey, mind running down to the garage and getting Mir? Tell her dinner's ready?" Poe asks, and Clay nods, heads out the door.

The yard dogs poke their triangle ears up as he passes, track him with their beady black eyes. They might not like him, but they know him. Know he's part of the pack.

Miri stays focused on the old Panhead she's building when Clay comes into the garage, doesn't look up. They're silent for a while, then Clay asks, "Why'd you skip school with that guy?"

"Why'd you follow us?" she shoots back.

Stupid! He tried to be invisible. And he didn't follow the *whole* time; he couldn't. After he'd tracked them to the old Gooch place—how did he not know somebody new was living there?—he'd had to get back to Paradise.

"Poe asked me to keep an eye on things," he says now.

"Did you tell him?"

"No."

"Thanks."

Clay shifts. He moves closer, hands Miri the open-end wrench when he notices that's what she's going to need next.

"Who is he anyway?" Clay asks.

"Fen. I told you."

"But who *is* he?"

"New kid. His dad moved here almost a year ago, I guess."

"Why?"

"Don't know—maybe the same reason Poe did at first. Some idea of getting back to nature, back to the land." She doesn't change expression, but starts speaking in a high falsetto. "'It's so beautiful here, so peaceful! So secluded!'"

Which cracks Clay up. An inside joke. A couple of tourists they ran into last summer, over at Hidden Waterfall. The knobs are isolated but sometimes you bump into random strangers, people hiking around, bird-watching, staring at trees in the fall—"the fall foliage," as the tourists say.

"'You're so lucky to live here.'" Miri does the same falsetto—the old lady with the wild white hair and the bird binoculars hanging from her neck and those ugly sandals on her feet, the ones that look like twine or rope is holding them together. "'So truly lucky.'"

Both of them are cracking up now, like it's the funniest thing in the world. Clay knows it's not, and Miri probably does too, but something's released. Maybe it's the beer for him, and for Miri, maybe it's knowing Clay didn't tell on her.

For whatever reason, it's like old times between them, easy. And of course Clay has an urge to lean close, try to kiss her again. But he doesn't. He won't make the same mistake he made before. He'll go slower, take his time. He'll explain to Miri how he feels, how he really feels. He'll talk it all through before he tries anything again. Because that's what Miri likes, talking about things. Like leaving. She talks and talks and talks about leaving, especially lately, and he wants to listen. And he also wants to be with her when she goes.

FEN

"How was school today?" his dad asks while they're choosing their nightly microwave dinners. Chicken enchilada for Fen and a Lean Cuisine Sweet Sriracha Braised Beef for his dad because he's always trying to lose a few pounds. (He ballooned up after he got sober and his cholesterol is always high.)

"Great!" Fen answers, and it's way too enthusiastic a response. Because his dad gives him that look—Detective Dad, Fen calls it. All zeroed in, focused and ready to listen, but also suspicious.

"Tell me about it," Detective Dad says, and Fen knows he'll have to give him something fact based.

"There were like five thousand kids in my last school, right?" Fen asks as if he expects his dad to know, and his dad falls into the trap, because he doesn't want to appear that he's basically been Absent Dad for the past few years.

"Right." His dad nods (fake) knowingly, slits the plastic wrapper on the top of Fen's frozen dinner, slides it into the microwave. "Easy to get lost."

"Well, this school's like three hundred kids, and that's all four grades, ninth through twelfth." Good thing that Fen had looked up the enrollment numbers online, soon as he knew he was moving here. "It's tiny! Almost like a private school!"

Maybe that's taking it a bit too far, because he's getting another Detective Dad look.

"I mean, obviously not. Nothing fancy about it. Obviously not a lot of rich kids—or *any* rich kids. Some of the kids seem kinda"—an image of camo dude Clay flashes through his brain—"rough. But others are"—Miri's body tucked close on the bike—"nice."

"And the classes, you think they'll be okay?" His dad is reaching into the fridge, pulling out two cold bottles of Ale-8-Ones, a soda made only in Kentucky that he's become addicted to down here (better than booze). "Enough of a challenge?"

"Classes are fine," Fen bluffs. "It's all good."

"Well, here's to fresh starts." His dad pops the tops off the two green bottles and hands one over. Fen actually thought the soda was beer when his dad first brought him here and he saw the empties in the kitchen corner. His stomach literally lurched. Drunk Dad had been much worse than any of the other Dad incarnations. "I'm proud of you, son." Clinking the neck of his bottle to Fen's. "You're settling right in."

"Thanks," Fen says, feeling only a tiny twinge of guilt for lying. And . . . maybe . . . he *is* settling in. He'll be starting school for real tomorrow. A shit hole, Miri had called it. But *she'd* be there, so how shitty could it be?

The microwave bings, and his dad goes to switch the dinners, burning his hands in the process—like always.

"You gotta wait for it to cool down," Fen tells him—like always.

"Yeah, yeah, yeah." His dad's usual impatient response. "I'm hungry." Going to the sink to run some cold water over his burned fingers. "Aren't you?" he asks. "Food wasn't so great at your *private school*, I'm betting." Chuckling at his own (non) joke.

"Yeah, pretty basic."

Plain cheese sandwiches to be exact. Filched from this very kitchen. All he could offer to make Miri when they came back up from the creek, both of them starving. She'd stayed on the porch (she didn't seem to want to come inside, and he couldn't blame her, though honestly the inside is surprisingly better than the outside) while he'd slapped a couple of American slices between some white bread. (His dad really has to get a better diet.)

"Where do you go to shop around here?" Fen had asked Miri while they were eating. "Because we definitely need some better supplies."

"We don't really shop a whole lot," she'd answered, seeming embarrassed about it. "We raise a lot of our own vegetables, we have chickens. And what we don't have, we trade for."

"Kinda back to the land?" Fen had asked.

"Something like that." She'd shrugged, gone on to explain about the closest Save A Lot (hour drive) and the Walmart (hour-and-a-half drive). "I'd make one big trip if I were you. Just like with the gas, it's good to stock up on food, on everything, really."

"Yeah, always good to stock up for the zombie apocalypse," he'd joked, but she'd seemed strangely serious when she'd mumbled, "For any kind of apocalypse."

"What else did you get up to today?" his dad is asking now that they both have their respective (nuked) dinners, sitting down across from each other at a scratched-up old wooden kitchen table that must've come with the place.

"Went for a walk," Fen says—again, good to stick to a line of truth. "Out back. There's a creek at the bottom of the hill. Did you know that?"

"Nope, haven't had a chance to look around much—haven't had time."

Which strikes Fen as odd, because he actually noticed his dad's boots on the back porch—caked in mud. Thought about borrowing them the next time he goes for a hike, though he does want to eventually get a pair of his own kick-ass boots, same as Miri's.

"Work's crazy right now," his dad continues while Fen's wolfing down his enchilada. He's never known his dad's work not to be "crazy."

"I heard meth's bad around here," Fen offers between bites, and he feels the switch—Detective Dad's back.

"You heard that at school?" He wipes some sriracha off his chin with a napkin, takes a gulp of Ale-8-One (which just tastes like a ginger-ale knockoff, in Fen's opinion).

"Some girl said a friend's mom got sent to prison." Again, the truth. Just not the whole truth.

Detective Dad nods his head knowingly. "It's one big vicious cycle." Same phrase he always uses when the conversation turns to the subject of drugs. "Hard to get out once you're in. The key is, never to get in." He points his fork at Fen. "Don't. Do. Drugs!" He jabs the fork in the air to emphasize each word.

"Yep, I think I got it. Thanks, Dad." Why'd he even go there?

"Your mom thought you were up to some funny business back in Detroit."

"'Funny business'?" He shakes his head. "Seriously, Dad, what century is that even from?"

"Which is pretty much why she sent you here." Ignoring Fen's comment, turning on the bad cop. "I'm going to give you the benefit of the doubt, son." Switching over to good cop. "I'm going to trust you. Don't prove me wrong."

"Yes, *sir*." More mocking, but it doesn't register.

"Good." Going all earnest dad-ness. "I'm really glad we had this talk, son."

"Yeah, Dad, me too."

Once the meal is over—it doesn't take too long to eat and clean up two microwave dinners—his dad says something about getting work done before bed and disappears into his room, which is fine by Fen.

Now he can download the stuff he recorded today, give it all a listen. He goes back to the first one, the "symphony of birds." He'll have to ask Miri about that ancient bell bird (if he ever lets her listen to what he records, which he probably won't). He knows he's waiting for the buzzing sound, the growl of Miri's engine, speeding closer and closer, louder and louder, and when it comes, he keeps hitting replay, but it always cuts out.

Too bad his finger automatically hit stop, too bad he didn't capture the rest—the screech of the tires, Miri's *What the hell?*

Fen closes his eyes, hits replay on the images inside his brain: the dark shape barreling toward him, the screech of tires. The utter surprise when the motorcycle swung back around, and it was not some dude behind the wheel, but Miri.

What the hell?

Fen can't believe he didn't get her cell number—although what's the point, right? He really has to talk to his dad about researching another phone plan, something that actually works around here.

Should he wait at the end of his driveway tomorrow morning for her motorcycle to come by so they can get to school at the same time?

Nah, that's lame. He's not a third grader. He doesn't need a bestie to walk to school with. Besides, he should leave the house early so he can do what she told him to—go to the BP station, gas up the truck, buy one of those plastic tanks and fill it up too. He doesn't want to get stranded again. Although, he has to admit, getting stranded this morning didn't turn out so bad.

CLAY

The thing about patrolling at night is that you can't let every little sound trip you up. The woods are alive after dark, and you've got to learn to separate what's out there doing its normal nighttime stuff from what might be out there making trouble.

Like now. There's some rustling going on to his right, a couple of yards off, but Clay knows it's most likely a skunk, digging around for roots to eat, showing its babies how to find food. So many babies in the woods right now. Skunks, raccoons, possums. He likes this time of year, likes how everything gets new again after dying off or holing up for winter.

Who cooks for you? Who cooks for you all?

A barred owl is calling across the ridge. Maybe the one he and Miri saved, who knows? Possibly a daddy now, or a mama—they never were able to tell because they didn't keep it long enough, just patched it up as best they could and let it go. Miri'd cried, but she understood. You can't keep anything wild. Not for long.

The male barred owl is generally smaller than the female. A pair will mate for life, and they'll take turns caring for their owlets—one going out hunting for mice or moles to feed the young, one guarding the nest. A baby owl will imprint on anything it sees when it first opens its eyes; that's what Clay's heard. Just like a duckling or a chick will do right after hatching.

Are you my mother?

The words pop into his head. A book, right? A silly book Poe used to read to Miri. Clay would pretend he was too old to be read to, but he'd linger after dinner, listen to Poe's deep, rumbly voice make the story seem less silly than it was.

A baby bird asking a cat, a car—even a bulldozer—the same question over and over again.

Are you my mother?

Clay never had to look for his mother. Before she went to prison, she was mostly always there—which wasn't necessarily a good thing. All those times she'd lie on the couch barely moving—days, nights—and he'd be so hungry, but there'd be nothing in the fridge, nothing in the cabinets. He'd tug on her arm, finally getting her to open her eyes. But she didn't see him.

Are you my mother?

Clay moves on through the dark. The rustling to his right stops, but only for a moment. The skunk, or whatever it is, knows Clay's there but clearly doesn't sense a threat. Clay is big, but he can make himself small in the woods. He can be invisible. Night or day, he can follow tracks, a trail left behind—animal or man. It seems like he grew up knowing how to do this, how to see patterns in a broken twig, a torn leaf, a shift in the dirt. Things that scream out to him are hidden to most people.

The boot prints Clay sees now, right this second, are not hidden. He squats down for a closer look.

Definitely boots. Good ones. Sturdy, rugged soles. Average size—eleven. Walking, not running. Taking it slow through the woods. Stopping, listening. Just like Clay has been doing. Up the hill, though, straight up. Not circling. One set of prints. Clay follows them along the ridge. Loses them for a moment in the brush, but picks up the trail again, follows it to the edge of the clearing.

Somebody stopped and watched here. The tracks are clear but not fresh. Clay squats down to finger their outline, and his thoughts go immediately to that kid Fen. But no. Bambi wasn't wearing boots; Clay doubts he even owns a pair.

The boots backtrack down the knob—Clay loses them over rock, a jagged ledge of shale. But he finds them again, boots sliding on the steep slope, hands grabbing onto hackberry branches for balance.

The county road loops up to its highest point here, and there's a place big enough for a truck to pull off and park. But the dirt's packed hard against the blacktop, and there's a scatter of gravel, too. So it's impossible to tell what kind of wheels this guy was driving.

Clay circles as he makes his way back up the knob, checking to be sure he didn't miss anything else, another set of prints. But all's clear—now at least. Whoever was sneaking around Paradise earlier is gone.

MIRI

She has a decision to make. Skip school again and let Fen face his first day alone without her so the buzzards have less to pick at. Or go to school and try to put a "fuck-off" protective shield around him. Which will probably backfire anyway. One whiff of Miri's interest in the new kid will for sure bring them all circling.

"Morning, sunshine."

Miri can't believe Angel's up at this hour, rooting around the kitchen.

"I'm making coffee," Angel says—another big surprise. "Want some?"

Miri hesitates. Obviously, this decision (to have coffee) should be a no-brainer compared to the whole Fen/school decision, but it suddenly all seems like too much.

"Where's Poe?" Miri asks, suspicious, avoiding a *yes* or *no* for the moment.

"Clay showed up super early." Angel is dumping the old coffee grounds into the compost pot, rinsing out the basket and drying it, filling it with new scoops. "Wanted to show your dad something that 'just couldn't wait.'"

"What was it?" Miri feels herself tensing up, thoughts jumping to Fen. Clay said he hadn't told Poe anything, but maybe he changed his mind. "Did Clay say?"

"You know how Clay is." Angel rolls her eyes. "Something to do with the woods, I don't know. Tracks or something."

Miri relaxes. "So why are *you* up?" She knows she's not her nicest self with Angel, and she's not exactly sure why. Angel tries so hard.

"Couldn't get back to sleep. Thought I'd make you some breakfast before you go to school, like Poe does."

"Poe doesn't even want me going to school," Miri says under her breath.

"Awww, sugar, he just wants what's best for you." Angel reaches out and gently tugs at a wayward strand of Miri's hair. "I've got some cute scrunchies in my room. You could borrow one. You have such a pretty face. You shouldn't hide it behind all that crazy hair."

Angel tries *too* hard. That's part of it. Especially with the aww-sugar-please-let-me-give-you-a-makeover thing. It gets old. If Miri wanted to bleach her hair blond and wear nothing but tank tops and short-shorts like Angel, she would.

"Thanks, but I'm good with coffee," Miri says. "Don't bother to make me anything. I'm not hungry." Did that come out too harsh? She starts to apologize, but Angel just sighs.

"Suit yourself." Turning away. "You always do," she says under her breath. "Maybe I'll try to get back to sleep after all." Heading down the hall—the bedroom she shares with Poe.

And maybe that's the other part of it. The fact that Angel and Poe are together, something she honestly doesn't get. Miri doesn't remember her mom at all—Miri was barely three when she died. But somehow she knows her mom wasn't a thing like Angel. Miri's seen one photo (only one, surprisingly; Poe's always said he was in too much of a fog leaving his old life behind to grab much), but in the photo, her mom has Miri's "crazy" hair and she appears to be wearing a baggy old T-shirt, the kind Miri prefers.

"You're just like your mom," Poe used to say all the time (pre-Angel), when Miri looked or acted a certain way. "Your mom would be so proud of you."

But would she be proud of Miri now? How she ignores so much. And what about Poe, the man she must have loved, the man she married and chose to have a baby with? Would she be proud of what Poe's become?

The coffeepot gives a final burst of gurgling, bringing Miri back to the kitchen. She pulls out the travel mug that attaches to her bike same as the water bottle, and fills it.

So, it's *yes* to coffee—one of the morning's dilemmas. She could still choose *no* for the Fen/school question. But that's not who she wants to be. And besides, she's not sure she can go a whole day without seeing Fen again. Strange, but true.

FEN

Okay, he needs to stop waiting for her. The motorcycle's not in the parking lot. Plus, who knows when she'll decide to show up—she was running late yesterday, right? That could be her MO. He, on the other hand, should not be late because it is, after all, his actual first day.

"Did you see the Pop-Tarts?" his dad called as he was rushing out for work even before Fen was out of bed. "They're in the cabinet next to the fridge."

"Yeah, thanks." Thinking how his mom would never in a million years buy Pop-Tarts for breakfast. (Talk about bad influences.)

Fen had taken a fair amount of time getting ready. He'd showered and then he'd shaved, which probably wasn't necessary. But the fuzz along his jaw comes in weirdly patchy if he doesn't watch it—obviously unlike Clay, with his nearly grown-ass man beard. How old did Miri say he was—couple of years older?

Anyway, Fen had kept to his black jeans and Chucks, but he went with a faded gray T-shirt because . . . well, he wasn't sure about the all-black thing here. It maybe seemed like . . . overkill. Plus, it was kinda hot. Sure, it was all black back at his old school, but Detroit seemed like a whole other planet at this point.

Going to the BP had taken longer than he expected. Some toothless old dude behind the counter hadn't seemed to understand at all when Fen asked where the two-gallon tanks were. And then it took forever to ring everything up and pay for it, and finally get back on the road to school.

Now Fen checks the time on his phone. He knows he has to bite the bullet and get out of the truck, make his way across the parking lot, past the dozen or so kids scattered across the front steps, half of them openly vaping. *Are you actually allowed to vape on school property here?*

"Here we go," he says to himself, and grabs the backpack, shoots out the door. He's turning to lock the truck when he finally hears that now-familiar buzzing, and he just manages to keep his cool. Doesn't spin back around and wave his arms in the air—something he'd honestly be in danger of doing if he didn't keep a firm grip.

The buzzing is deepening into a growl as she gets closer. It's only when he knows for sure Miri's in the next parking spot over that he finishes up the (extra-long) task of making sure the truck is locked.

"Hey," he says, turning, as if he's just realized she's there.

"Hey," she echoes, but she's not meeting his eye. Not a good sign. Fen's heart takes a tiny nosedive. What's up? Everything seemed fine yesterday—a whole lot better than fine, actually.

"Did you get gas?" Miri asks, still not looking his way. He watches her go through all the motions he somehow already knows by heart—shifting the motorcycle onto its kickstand, switching off the motor, swinging her leg over.

"Yeah, I filled up at the BP." He hikes his thumb toward the back. "And I got a two-gallon like you said."

"Good." Now she's eyeing the front steps, and he follows her gaze. Is he imagining it, or is everyone suddenly all perked up, staring back at them like he and Miri have suddenly sprouted horns or something?

"I guess it's too late for us to skip, huh?"

Did she really just say that?

"We could make a run for it."

Did he really just say that back?

"Nah. Might as well get it over with."

Now Miri *is* looking at him, and it's like they've gone back to yesterday, sitting beside the creek, easy and . . . right.

"We're in this shit hole together," he tells her, and they're not holding hands as they walk across the parking lot, but it feels like they might as well be.

CLAY

He keeps an ear out for the buzz of the Sportster. Five o'clock, six—he checks the old clock hanging in his kitchen—but Miri's still not home.

Clay steps out onto the rickety porch attached to his trailer. Maybe he'll just go on down to the old Gooch place, check to make sure she's with Bambi, check to make sure she's okay. Make sure she's not busted all to pieces skidding on the wet road—storm coming up fast like it did in the midafternoon, exactly the time Miri got out of school.

She's careful, though—Clay knows this. Even before she had the Bambi option (which he doesn't like, not at all), she'd stop for heavy rain, take shelter under a ledge, under some trees if she had to. She wouldn't risk wrecking herself, yeah, but she definitely wouldn't risk wrecking her bike.

There are girls who love horses—it's Kentucky, after all. Girls who just want to be with horses all the time, brush them, braid their manes and tails, love on them. But Miri's not like that. Or maybe she is, though it's not a horse she's crazy about, a living creature, but a machine. Metal and steel, chrome and leather. Old bike parts she puts together to make something new, just because she can.

Baby Wizard.

That's what he'd call her sometimes when they were little. Because she could fix anything on two wheels (or four), same as the Wizard himself, same as Poe, who earned the nickname from the bikers who started trickling up the knob in search of that crazy mechanic with the magic touch. Bikers who later started finding their way up to Paradise for something else.

"What's that?" Clay remembers Miri asking one day. Poe had run to the house for something, and she'd gone ahead and jacked open the crankcase on a bike some guy had left to be fixed. Clay had glanced over, noted all the tiny packets of crystal.

"Crank." Without even thinking about it. Crank, meth, crystal— whatever you wanted to call it—was common as fleas on a dog in the knobs.

"That's a crank*case*," Miri had said, correcting him, acting like a know-it-all.

"Yeah, and that's why it's called *crank*, dummy."

Her eyes nearly popped out of her head at that. He'd never called her dummy before, and immediately he'd regretted it.

"What is?"

"This." He'd put a finger to one of the tiny plastic pillows, then pulled his hand back and closed the lid fast when he glimpsed Poe coming back to the garage. "Don't tell your dad you saw it," he whispered. "He'll be mad."

Miri had obeyed, far as he knew. And Poe had kept her in the dark, mostly. But then Angel had arrived, and business seemed to really explode.

When Miri started going to school instead of Poe homeschooling her, guys would come up to her in the hallways, ask if she was holding, ask if she could get them a special discount—that's what she'd told Clay later.

"Does Poe make it?" she'd asked Clay then. "Does he . . . *cook* it?"

And Clay had been amazed all over again. How . . . clueless Miri still was, how naive—was that the word? He wasn't that much older, and yet he felt ancient right then, old as the knob itself.

"Ask him yourself," he'd told her, and stalked away, mad for no reason he could name.

Clay starts down the steps now, ready to head into the woods, down to the old Gooch place. Just to check. But before he makes it out of the clearing, he hears the buzz of the Sportster's motor—far off, but getting closer, winding its way back up the knob.

MIRI

She knows he's there before he says anything, but she keeps her back to him, stays focused on her bike, checking the engine bolts because there was a rattle as she came around the last turn.

"Poe was looking for you before," Clay says finally.

"When?"

"After the storm whipped up."

"It wasn't so bad," she tells him. "Probably worse up here."

"Poe was worried."

Somehow she knows Clay is lying. Poe doesn't really worry about her. He gets all worked up about imaginary black helicopters, yells at her to stay home from school sometimes, but he doesn't worry about normal things.

"I just had to wait the rain out a little," she says, and she wants Clay to ask her where she waited—at Fen's place; she wants to tell him, wants to get it over with.

"Tell Poe I'm not coming to supper tonight," he says after a while. "I need to start patrolling early."

That's when Miri does turn. "What are you patrolling for anyway?" But the doorway's empty; Clay's already gone.

FEN

Even with the advance warning, he was still holding out hope that Miri was wrong, or at least exaggerating. But no. School here's definitely a shit hole.

"How've you survived all these years?" Fen asks after a full week of sitting through some astoundingly dumbed-down classes; some seriously hostile looks from just about every kid (male or female) in each and every class—what's up with *that*?

"I didn't always go there," Miri explains. They're sitting on a ledge—way high up, different knob—he's gotten used to the word. A favorite place Miri wanted to show him. Every day after school, they've either hung on his porch (still staying outside), or they've jumped on her bike (his favorite thing to do), and she's basically been his own personal tour guide.

"You mean there's another option?" he asks, nudging at her. "Have you been holding out on me?"

"Not really. But there's always home school. That's what I did up until a few years ago."

He blinks. "So, why'd you stop?"

"It's complicated."

Same thing she said that first day.

"What's complicated about staying home and never having to go back to that shit hole again?"

Okay, wow. He meant it as a joke, but it didn't exactly come out that way, and he's about to apologize, but he also braces himself. He's barely known Miri a week, but he's seen how her eyes flash at some of the kids at school. And he hasn't forgotten how she laid into Clay, semiautomatic and all.

"I don't want to stay home, okay?" Her eyes *are* flashing and her voice *is* raised, but she's not jumping up and running off.

"Sorry." Tentatively, he reaches out, takes her hand. "Didn't mean to be an asshole. I just wish we could . . . I don't know . . . homeschool together . . . or something."

He waits for her to jerk her hand away, but she doesn't. In fact, she adjusts her grip so their palms are pressed flat, fingers weaving together. They've been close on the bike, obviously, super close. But this is the first time they've actually held hands, and it's making all these jangly things happen inside his body.

"Would your dad"—he clears his throat because it's suddenly closed tight—"would *Poe* want to homeschool us both?" Giving her a sideways glance and a half grin. "What'd'ya think?"

"Yeah, that's going to happen." She rolls her eyes, but she's grinning, too, revealing that tiny gap he's kinda nuts about. "Here's the thing," she says, obviously making a decision, going serious.

"We moved to the knobs when I was three, and Poe was all about getting back to the land, like I mentioned. But then he met this old couple. Junie and Cyrus. They live over on one of the other knobs, and they're, like, old hippies because they grow and raise all their own food, make everything themselves—which is totally cool! But they're also big survivalists. And they got Poe into it too."

"Survivalist . . . like conspiracy-theory-take-over-the-government survivalist?"

"A bit of that," Miri admits. "But it's more about . . . stockpiling, getting ready for something really bad to happen. Making sure you're prepared for"—checking in with him—"the *zombie* apocalypse."

"Or"—reading the look—"*any* kind of apocalypse, right?"

"Right!" Nodding, mock impressed. "Anyway, June and Cyrus gave Poe this book. *How to Survive the End of the World as We Know It.*" She winces. "Yeah, that's the actual title. But it was Poe's bible for a while, so it became *my* bible. And that's a lot of what he taught me at home school. How to survive 'when the shit hits the fan' . . . or WTSHTF as the author calls it in his book."

"WTF?" Fen jokes. "But seriously, what kind of stuff did you learn?"

"Like how to hunt and fish, live in the woods if I had to. I learned all about which kinds of plants or berries you can eat." She gives him a quick look. "I even know what kinds of bugs give you the best protein."

"Okay . . ." Grimacing. "Not sure I could handle that."

"You'd be surprised. Some bugs really aren't so bad." She pauses. "Take the stink bug, for instance. Once you get past the name—and the smell!—it's actually kind of yummy. Has a fruity taste—almost like apples."

He stares at her. Is she serious or just messing with him?

"Hey, I nearly forgot! I happen to have a baggie of dried stink bugs in case we need a snack." She starts to reach for her backpack, but that's when she gives it away, eyes flashing—playful, not angry.

"Okay, you got me! You *so* got me!" Scowling, but pulling her closer. Suddenly he's dying to kiss her, but is it too soon?

"Poe also taught me self-defense," Miri is saying, and yeah, it's too soon.

"So, you could beat the shit out of me?" Fen jokes.

"Probably." Flexing a muscle. "I'm stronger than I look. And I'm pretty handy with a gun. Because that's a big part of the stockpiling thing. Poe has lots of guns. Lots. And I know how to shoot them—all of them—take them apart, clean them, put them back together again."

Of course Fen's thoughts rush to Clay, the AR-whatever he was carrying. Makes more sense now. If Clay's their neighbor, he's probably into the whole survivalist thing too. Still, it doesn't totally explain how trigger-happy he seemed, how eager to order Fen to raise his hands in the air.

"The thing is, I like hunting." Miri glances tentatively at him—does she think he'll disapprove? "I mean, I don't *love* killing animals, but I do feel that if you're hunting for a reason—to put food on your table—it's justifiable. If you're really respectful—don't take any more than you absolutely need—and use everything, every bit of the animal."

"I get that." Fen nods. "I've done some hunting. In fact, my dad keeps talking about all these hunting trips we're supposed to take down here . . . if he ever makes the time."

"Maybe we could go together sometime," Miri suggests, still a little tentative.

"Sure." He nods again. "I'd like that."

"Anyway, it's not like that's all Poe taught me, crazy survivalist stuff." She rolls her eyes. "He taught me how to read and write, do math and science. He used to collect all these old books, and he'd read them to me every night at bedtime. Shakespeare—pretty much all the plays, though I think I fell asleep a lot. *The Odyssey. A Tale of Two Cities. Frankenstein*—which was my favorite book, by the way. Still is. *Jane Eyre, Wuthering Heights.* Oh, and *Moby Dick* . . . that one took a really, really long time."

Fen raises an eyebrow. "So . . . no *Cat in the Hat* at bedtime for you, huh?"

Acting offended. "Dr. Seuss was a big part of the curriculum too!"

"*Sneetches* was an existential masterpiece ahead of its time."

"Clearly." Miri does reach over into her backpack now, pulling out her water bottle (not any dried bug snacks). "And, of course, I learned a lot about fixing things," she says as they take turns drinking. "Poe used to fix bikes for people, so I'd just learn by watching him all day long."

"Seems like you and Poe are close."

"We *were*."

Fen waits for more, but Miri stays silent, and he doesn't push it. They have time. All the time in the world, right?

"Hey, are those hawks out there?" he asks after a moment, lifting his chin toward the big black birds—a pair of them—that have been circling lazily (and silently) in the distance since he and Miri first got here.

"Buzzards." Miri takes a drink of water. "And . . . that's what I call the kids at school. Buzzards."

"Buzzards." Pondering. "Same thing as vultures?"

"Pretty much."

"Okay, yeah. I can see that." Nodding. "Which reminds me—something that's been bugging me all week. I always thought people in the South were supposed to be nice. Southern hospitality and all that."

"Everything's different in the knobs," she tells him. "People keep to themselves. Always have. That's why there's more than one—or three—survivalists. It's remote. Perfect place to hole up and wait until—"

"The shit hits the fan," Fen finishes, taking her hand again, palms tight together like before.

"Yeah. TSHTF." She grins over at him—that gap!—and he's thinking how it's already too late. The shit has *already* hit the fan, and there's nothing he can do about it.

MIRI

Poe's been making bread. The smell hits her as soon as she walks through the door. Big and round and comforting. Totally at odds with the sight of the man himself, sitting at the dining room table, old newspapers spread before him, a bunch of guns laid out on top of that.

"Wanna help clean these?" he asks right away.

Miri can't believe she was just telling Fen about all this, and now here it is.

"Why?" she asks, though she knows the answer. Guns, like cars or bikes, can't just stay idle or they'll freeze up.

"The Governor needed some TLC, so thought I'd just go ahead and do the rest." The Smith and Wesson .45 Governor is Poe's favorite; it goes everywhere with him, usually tucked under his shirt at the back of his waistband. Angel always puts on a thick Cockney accent when referring to "the Guv'nor." "Rimfire there's been missing you," Poe says, his voice floating in a singsong.

The Smith and Wesson Rimfire used to be her favorite handgun, the one she'd use the most for target practice out back, but she hasn't handled it in a while. "I don't think guns have feelings." She's moving through the house, hiking open as many windows as she can. The sharp aroma of solvent, lubricant, is nearly choking out the yummy bread smell.

"We could go out and do some target practice," Poe offers. "Just you and me. You're probably getting rusty."

"I'm hungry." Miri heads for the kitchen now—four loaves already waiting on the warming rack and one still in the oven. She wishes she could just grab a whole loaf, take it back to her room. Avoid talking to Poe. But she knows he'd get all stormy. She takes out the serrated bread knife, slices a couple of pieces, and downs them right away.

"Just got some butter from Junie and Cyrus," Poe says. "Traded some transmission work on the old Plymouth for it."

"How's June doing?" Miri asks, mouth still full. She pulls the butter out from the fridge, the blue ceramic crock made by Cyrus in his kiln. Miri hasn't been to visit for a while, but she knows June's arthritis always flares up in the heat.

"She's getting by," Poe says. "Misses seeing you."

A pang of guilt. Miri wonders if she could take Fen with her on a visit. Since she's been showing him all her favorite spots, since she's already told him about the end-of-the-world crap. Is it crap? Miri's not sure. One of the reasons she needs to get out of here eventually. So she can get a different perspective. So she can really see. She told Clay she wants to go to the desert because she's tired of trees. A metaphor maybe? (Poe taught her about metaphors long before she got to the shit hole school.) She's tired of all the branches, all the leaves here in the knobs, all the clutter that keeps her from seeing things as they really are.

"Hey, pull out that last loaf," Poe calls to her. "Should be done by now."

Miri opens the stove door, and sure enough the bread looks perfect—the crust a golden brown—so she slides on the big oven mitts, pulls out the heavy Dutch pan Poe uses, and sets it on the range. It takes some muscle to turn the pan over, flip the bread upside down onto one of the cooling racks.

"Be careful," Poe says. "Don't burn yourself."

Miri rolls her eyes, flips the bread like she's done hundreds of times. She wonders if Fen's ever had fresh bread. At a bakery, sure—there are probably lots of bakeries in Detroit. At home, though? Straight out of the oven? From what Fen's said, Miri doesn't get the impression that his dad—or mom—cooks a whole lot. She wishes Fen were here, right this minute.

"Bring me some, darlin'? If you don't mind?" Poe calls. "Got my hands full."

Miri slices up the rest of the loaf and slathers on thick layers of June's butter—the way she knows Poe likes it.

"Here you go." Setting the plate on the table—an empty space between the Smith and Wesson Rimfire and the Pro.

"Thanks, hon." His eyes find hers—not lasering this time, not storming, just normal dad eyes. Crinkles at the corners. More than there used to be. Gray hair taking over his brown sideburns. He was a lot younger—they both were—when he took her out to the place in the woods where they always went for target practice.

She'd basically been shooting BB guns since she could stand, rifles when she was old enough to go hunting.

But the Rimfire was different, lighter than a rifle, fitting in one hand. No stock tucked into her shoulder; no arm-length barrel to sight. But the breathing was the same, the need to steady that breathing, slow it down but keep things flowing through the shot.

"I knew you'd get it right away," Poe had told her when she hit her mark first round. "You're a natural."

And she still remembers how happy that made her, how proud. Back then she'd wanted to be just like Poe. The way he handled guns, the way he fixed bikes, the way he talked and moved. Those mix-and-match eyes, and all that ink swirling down her arms—full sleeve tattoos, shoulder to wrist. A coat of many colors, a puzzle of interlocking pieces. Ocean waves and fish morphing into birds and clocks, moon and stars. Wheels and winding roads, of course. Roses and thorns. Guns. And more than one skull.

Miri used to take Sharpies and draw up and down her own arms. She used to beg Poe to let Scratch, the traveling tattoo guy who comes up the knob every few months, put a flower or a bird or a star, one small thing, right there on her own skin. But Poe always said no, said she could make that choice when she was older.

"Scratch'll be making the rounds soon," Poe says like he's reading her mind—something Clay believes Poe can actually do because of his mismatched eyes. "You're nearly seventeen. If you want some ink, I'm not going to stop you."

"Not sure what I'd get." Miri turns away, goes back into the kitchen, where she grabs another slice of bread to take to her room. She needs to be alone.

"Well, you have some time to think about it," Poe calls after her.

"Okay," she responds, though in truth she doesn't need any time to think about it. She doesn't want a tattoo. Not anymore. Clay has a couple—a cross, though she's never known him to go to church; an owl for the baby they found in the woods. Angel has a bunch, but her pride and joy are the wings flared open across her back (a kind of obvious choice, if you ask Miri).

Miri's only seen Fen's pale neck and arms, those strangely beautiful feet. But she doubts he has a line of ink on him, and she decides she wants to be like that—unmarked, pure.

CLAY

Poe is back to using one of those high-tech handhelds. Military grade. Basically a walkie-talkie but with a thousand-mile radius.

"Keep it on the channel I've programmed it to," Poe reminded him before Clay started out on tonight's patrol. "We won't have to worry about other folks listening in."

He begins at the bottom of the knob this time. Where he found the tire marks. Still visible when he showed Poe but gone now. Nothing taking their place.

But he does find another set of tracks, same boots from before, after he's crossed over to where the creek feeds in from the old Gooch place.

Again, his thoughts fly first to Bambi, but again, all he's seen him wear are those dumb-ass Converse.

He knows Miri is spending every afternoon with Bambi. He needs to talk to her about that; he doesn't trust the guy, though he doesn't think he's the prowler. Probably the prowler is some rival of Poe's, somebody who wants to spy on his operation, maybe even try a takeover, which would be stupid. Poe's got leverage in lots of different places. Clay doesn't understand it all, but he doesn't have to. Not until Poe thinks he's ready. Or until Miri really decides to leave, whichever comes first.

Clay glances up, notices the moon is bigger tonight, a lot of it blocked by the trees that Miri hates so much right now. Still, the light spilling along the ground is brighter, everything more defined. A raccoon crosses a few feet away, between two cracked logs, and then three babies follow. Clay squints into various branches as he passes, wishing he could see the big puffed-out outline of the barred owl, wishing he could hear the call again. But the owl is silent. Maybe he—if it is a he—has found a mate.

He stops short. Has Miri found a "mate"? A coldness surges through him, but he tamps it down. Sadness, anger—any emotion—gets in the way of tracking, and that's his job right this moment.

Clay's been leaving Miri alone lately, letting her have her space. Not because he wants to. But because he knows it's the right thing to do.

Sometimes when you're hunting, you don't go after your target right away—there's no skill in that. You keep your distance, observe for a while, get to know the way an animal thinks, moves; what it startles at, what makes it calm. Once you think you understand the creature you're tracking, then you can zero in.

FEN

"You don't get claustrophobic, do you?"

"Don't think so," Fen answers, though he's not totally sure.

Miri's ahead of him on another skinny deer path through the woods—funny he's never actually spotted any deer on any of these hikes—but she stops to glance back over her shoulder.

"It gets a little tight, but then it opens up, I swear." Her eyes are flashing—playful again.

"What opens up?"

But she doesn't answer. She simply spins back around and drops to her knees. Then she's gone. Just like that.

What the hell?

Fen sprints forward, and that's when he sees what he didn't before: a rocky outcropping, mostly hidden by weeds and brush. Squatting down, he gets a strong whiff of dank, musty dark. A good-sized hole in the ground—possibly a tunnel—that's how Miri pulled off the disappearing act.

"Okay . . ." He runs a hand through his hair, glances back down the deer path, scanning the trees, the ridgeline. Nobody in sight, of course. What did he expect? They never see a soul on these treks of theirs, though sometimes Fen has the weirdest feeling they're being watched.

"You coming?" Miri's voice echoes out from the hole, sounding miles away already. "What's the holdup?"

"No holdup!" he yells back, and then before he can analyze it too much, he's on all fours, crawling forward into the dark like some animal. A bear burrowing deep into the earth, hibernating for winter.

At first there's a bit of light filtering in behind him, but soon the world goes pitch-black. Eyes open or shut—it makes no difference. The temperature drops, almost like the place is air-conditioned. Not so bad, honestly, since it was pretty hot and sticky out there in the sun. And he's actually getting used to the musty smell. At first he thought he'd sneeze and keep sneezing, but the urge passed. He can hear water dripping somewhere up ahead; he can hear his own breathing—a little jagged from crawling in a small space. He wants to slide his phone out of his front pocket, hit record. But what if he dropped it? Would he be able to find it again?

"You made it! You're here!"

The tunnel's suddenly opened up—he can feel it, even if he still can't see—and Miri's got hold of one arm, helping him to stand, steadying him over uneven ground.

"Where's here?" he asks, blind, blinking.

"It's a cave. Part of a string of caves. This is the biggest chamber."

"Cool." His voice, both their voices, are deep, echoey—nice sound.

Miri is leading him to some kind of rock ledge—he can feel it at the back of his knees—and they ease down together.

"Hey, there's a flashlight on my phone," Fen says, starting to reach for it, but Miri stops him.

"Wait. Your eyes will adjust. Humans rely too much on light. We can't see in the dark as well as animals, but we're not as helpless as we think."

He's not sure he buys that. Maybe Miri has some kind of see-in-the-dark superpower that he simply doesn't possess. But slowly things *do* start to shift, change. Not like a sudden spotlight shining down, but a lifting, a thinning of the shadows.

"Cool," he repeats, truly meaning it this time. "Cool."

She's still holding on to his arm, and she slides her hand down, finds his, palms together, their "thing" now.

"How'd you even discover this place?" he asks. "How'd you know it was here?"

"Clay showed me."

A tiny jolt—jealousy? Maybe. Miri seems to drop Clay's name a fair amount. But she's here with *Fen*, right? She's holding *his* hand.

"We used to come here a lot when we were younger," she adds, which makes him feel better. Miri and Clay grew up together, they're neighbors—no big deal. "And learning about caves and how they formed around here—that was part of Poe's home school."

"So . . . how'd they form around here?" Fen asks.

"Well, for one thing, Kentucky is karst country," Miri answers, and the phrase makes him laugh even though he has no idea what she's talking about.

"Bet you can't say that three times fast," he jokes. "Kentucky is karst country." And they both try, but it's impossible, so they give up.

"Karst is the type of topography we have in Kentucky," Miri clarifies. "Full of holes, shifting. Porous. The rock is mostly limestone, which is soft. Basically it's because all this was an ocean." She sweeps an arm out. "Like millions of years ago. Most of Kentucky. It was all underwater."

"So . . . if we time-traveled to prehistoric days, we'd be swimming right now?"

"Doing the backstroke."

"I like that."

"Me too."

He wants to lean in close, kiss her. It feels like the right moment.

"I used to come down here when I was little." Miri starts talking, and he decides to wait. "And I used to imagine all these sea creatures swimming around." Her voice has gone to a whisper, like they're in a library or a sacred place, and maybe they are. "Poe would have me do rubbings with a pencil and paper. Fossils on the walls, embedded in rock. Tiny shells and skeletons, proof that there was life down here before us. Proof that everything changes, that nothing stays the same."

Fen closes his eyes. He likes how Miri's voice echoes, even in a whisper. He likes how the slow dripping of water doesn't stop, just keeps going. Like a clock, like time itself. A slow, steady beat. Without thinking, he reaches into his pocket for his phone.

"You really don't need your flashlight," Miri says, not whispering so much anymore, sounding slightly annoyed, so he knows he has to come clean.

"I record stuff," he confesses before he can change his mind.

"Everyday stuff. Ambient sound, that's what it's called. Like traffic in the city—cars and sirens and people walking and talking." He pauses, waiting for her to react, pull her hand politely away. But she doesn't. So he keeps going. "Usually, I'm working with urban sounds—never been that into nature before. But it's great here. I'm liking it. A lot. I'm recording all these crazy birdcalls—never knew there were so many different birds! And squirrels—had no idea they made this weird chirping sound, didn't know they made *any* sound at all! Always thought they were just, I don't know, *silently* gathering their nuts for the winter, or whatever."

"*That's* what you were doing!" Miri cries out. "Those times I thought you were checking your phone, seeing if you were getting service!"

"Busted."

Miri laughs. "I just thought you were this city boy who couldn't live without his phone."

"Well, that's partially true," Fen admits. "I'd hate to lose my phone, because that's how I record everything. And then I transfer it all to my laptop and take certain tracks and mix them together, create this . . . collage. That's what some people call it, because it's not like I'm the only one in the whole world doing this. A collage of sound. Or a soundscape—like a painting, like a *land*scape, but with sound."

"Painting with sound," Miri repeats. "I like that." She pauses. "Can I hear one of your soundscapes? Can you play me one now?"

"No, sorry. I just have the raw stuff on my phone—what I've recorded," he explains, glad it's actually true. Telling Miri about his hobby, his obsession—whatever it is—is one thing, but letting her listen . . . He's not sure he's ready for that yet. "The rest's at home."

Miri nods. "There aren't any birds or squirrels down here. What do you want to record, anyway?"

"Your voice, for one," he admits. "When you were talking about the ocean and fossils and time . . . and karst! There's this great echo down here."

Now he does feel her pull away the tiniest bit, so he switches gears. "But I don't have to record you. I know that might be weird—making you repeat things into my phone. And some people hate the sound of their own voice when they hear it played back. But there's lots to record down here. Like that water dripping sound, the water dripping from somewhere . . ." He lets his voice drift off.

"Yeah, there's a spring that feeds into this cave." Miri is back to whispering. "Never goes dry, even in the middle of summer." They both listen for a while, then she squeezes his hand again, releases it. "Go ahead." Nudging his shoulder. "I'll stay quiet. I won't say a word."

"It'll just take a couple of minutes, I swear," he says, and she nods again.

Fen unlocks the phone, opens the app, and hits record . . . and yeah, it's kinda awkward, he has to admit. He's never had somebody sit right next to him and listen while he's recording. At first, his thoughts are flying all over the place—is the dripping water such a great sound? Will Miri get bored? Does she think he's crazy?

But after a moment or two, the sound starts taking over, like it always does for him. There's a soft, slow *drip . . . drip . . . drip*. And then there's a louder *drop, drop, drop* he didn't notice before. The two different beats are at odds at first, but then they are coming together, merging, melding. A new sound. A new rhythm—almost like a heartbeat. Like some giant creature is down here with them; some giant *sea* creature. And it's swimming through the ocean that used to be here, gulping Fen and Miri up, swallowing them whole.

"Okay," he says after he's hit the stop button. How long has it been? He can't tell. It could've been a few minutes or it could've been hours. That's the way it is when he loses himself in it all. He hopes it wasn't too long; he hopes he didn't bore Miri to death. "Sorry!" He tucks the phone away. "Didn't meant to geek out there."

"No, it was . . . cool. It made me listen to things . . . closer. Deeper."

"Yeah! That's exactly how it is when I'm recording, like I'm hearing things a lot *deeper* than normal."

"I've been in this cave hundreds of times . . ."

With Clay. He can't help it.

". . . but I guess I've never really *listened*."

"Most people don't," Fen tells her. "Most people don't hear things. Like, *really* hear them. They think they do, but they just . . . don't."

"Yeah," she says softly. And then she's the one leaning in, leaning all the way in, and her lips are touching his, and for once in his life, all sound fades away.

MIRI

"There you are!" Poe says as soon as she walks through the door. "Where've you been all this time? You're late!"

Miri can't answer straight off. Her brain is fuzzy and her lips are—she puts a hand to her mouth—tender, bruised.

But that's just how they *feel*, right? They don't *look* any different. Nothing Poe—or Clay, if he's here—would notice.

"My chain was sagging," Miri manages finally. "Took me some time to adjust it." Not a total lie. The chain on her bike *is* loose. But now she's got to remember to fix it before Poe notices.

"Well, we've been waiting"—Poe's sitting next to Angel at the dining table—"like one pig waits for another!" An old joke. Pigs don't wait if they've got food in front of them.

I'm not hungry. What she wants to say. But she knows trying to bypass food and go straight to her room—along with being late in the first place—would send up all kinds of red flags.

"Where's Clay?" she asks, noticing he's not at the table.

"Kid said he wasn't hungry—again," Poe grumbles. "Something's up, I can feel it. Clay's been distracted." He glances toward Miri. "Any ideas on what's going on?"

"He's fine." Miri crosses to the kitchen so she can wash her hands. She stands at the sink, watching the cave mud detach itself from her fingers, swirl down the drain.

It was so hard to say goodbye to Fen, after they'd finally made it outside again, kissing some more before splitting apart, heading home. She was glad it had been dark—just in case Clay was watching, tracking her like she knows he's done a couple of times already. Weird that Clay's kiss—Miri's first ever—happened only a couple of weeks ago. She'd felt guilty—still feels guilty—but now she understands. What it feels like to kiss somebody and not want to stop.

"Better get your ass on over here!" Angel's already slurring a little—not unusual at dinner. "Or there won't be any left!" She has a couple of cans of Country Boy Cougar Bait next to her plate. One down, more to go, probably. "Poe made your favorite, just for you."

"Great," Miri says, taking a seat. "Thanks." Poe slides the big serving bowl—half full of pesto gnocchi—across the table, but Angel intercepts it.

"Here you go, sugar." Heaping an enormous spoonful onto Miri's plate, as if she's a little kid, can't serve herself.

"Thanks," she mutters, then takes a bite because she knows she has to—Poe's watching. "It's good," she says, though in truth, she's not even tasting it. "Really good."

"Glad you like it," Poe says. "And there's plenty. Besides this. I made an extra batch. Put it in the freezer so you'll have it when you want it."

Miri's fork stops midair. "Going somewhere?" Trying to sound casual.

Freezing food is what Poe does when he's going on a trip—as if Miri and Angel can't cook for themselves, as if they'll starve on their own.

"Little trip," Poe answers. "Just a coupla days. Three at the most."

Miri puts the gnocchi into her mouth, chews. Potatoes mashed inside little pasta pillows, tossed in pesto—perfect comfort food. She used to call it *yesc*chi when she was little because she loved it so much. *Yesc*chi instead of *gno*cchi.

"Angel's coming with. So, you'll be on your own this time."

Miri looks up, surprised. Poe usually takes these "little trips" alone.

"Hope you're not gonna be scared all by yourself." Angel reaches out and pats Miri's arm. Her nails are raw, bitten down to the quick, a "nasty habit" she'll say herself, usually something she hides under bright, glittery glue-ons.

"Why would I be scared? This is my home."

"I'd get spooked here." Angel shrugs. "If I was all by my lonesome."

"I'll be fine." Miri glances to Poe again. "And anyway, Clay will be here, right?" Trying once more to sound totally casual. "He's not going with you, is he?"

"Nope. Clay'll keep an eye on things. If he gets his head outta whatever kinda cloud he's in right now." Poe's eyes ignite, go laser. "Any idea what's up with that kid lately?" he asks again.

Miri shakes her head, focuses on trying to eat a few more bites. "He's not a kid." *And he's not your kid.* She wishes Clay would get that, leave Poe to his "business," take off and never look back. It's what she'll do—when she's old enough.

"I'm going to set you up with one of the handhelds before I go," Poe says, rising from the table, starting to stack his and Angel's dishes, the serving bowl. "I've already given one to Clay. He's going to check in every day, and I want you to do the same. And you know with the handheld, you can always reach me, but—"

"No one can listen in," Miri finishes. Same old same old. Miri hasn't used a fancy walkie-talkie in a while, but she hasn't forgotten. A whole section of her home-school lesson plan was devoted to communicating off the grid. It's the reason they've never owned a phone—cell or landline. Their limited (at least for Miri) TV and internet is thanks to satellite. "When you leaving?" Again, she tries to sound like she couldn't care less.

"Tomorrow. We'll load up the truck after you take off for school."

"Where you going?" Miri's not sure why she's even asking. Sometimes Poe will bring back random bike parts—or a whole bike, something vintage, rare—after one of these little trips. But lots of times he comes back empty-handed. And he never tells her where he's been.

He shrugs before turning, heading for the kitchen. "'Don't ask me no questions,'" he sings over his shoulder, the chorus of some old rock classic she can't remember the name of, "'. . . won't tell you no lies.'"

FEN

"Where to today?"

The last bell has finally rung, and they're walking across the parking lot to their respective getaway vehicles. Miri's tugging at his hand—something she doesn't usually do with the buzzards watching—to speed things along. They'd brushed lips a few times today—hiding in the hallway between classes, ducking behind the shelves in the (minuscule) library, but he's dying to kiss her for real.

"My place." Miri's eyes are mischief-flashing and her (gorgeous) gap is showing. "Poe's gone for a coupla days."

Fen's heart does this weird little flip. It's not like he and Miri have never been alone; they're alone all the time. But this is different. Going to Miri's place is like sneaking out in the middle of the night back in Detroit. Kinda risky, but irresistible.

"I'll follow behind like usual," Miri says. "Pick you up at your house. I'm not sure about your truck in our driveway."

"Right."

"Oh, and bring your laptop," she says before getting on the bike. "I want to hear some of those soundscapes."

He's about to say no—still not sure about sharing them, at least not yet. But she's already kick-starting the engine.

When they get to his house, he thinks maybe Miri will forget, but she calls after him as he heads into the house to dump his stuff, so he goes ahead and grabs the mixing laptop and sticks it in its backpack case. He stops in the bathroom to check his hair, brush his teeth—fresh and minty!—and then he ducks outside and practically leaps onto the back of the bike.

Halfway down the obstacle course that is Miri's driveway, Fen *does* have a PTSD moment imagining Clay jumping out from behind a tree, shouting at him to raise his hands in the air.

But there's no literal stickup this time, and the driveway actually smoothes out at some point, turning to gravel. Fen catches sight of a couple of basic outbuildings, and then the house itself is rising out of the clearing—all angles and glass and natural wood. Not in the least what he was expecting.

"Poe built it himself," Miri calls over her shoulder, reading his mind.

"Awesome!" Fen says, thinking how his place is a total dump compared to this.

Miri parks next to a large, open-door garage—Fen counts at least eight motorcycles inside, maybe more; lots of tools lining the walls. She cuts the engine and they both slide off. He's about to ask her to show him which bike she's rebuilding—the new one she's mentioned. But before he can get a word out, the world explodes—a frenzy of barking. Not just one dog, even two. A whole pack—crazed, rabid. Terrifying.

"Sorry!" Miri yells over the noise, and before he can grab her, maybe pull her to the garage for safety, she's already striding around the corner of the garage, heading straight for . . .

Pit bulls. He sees them now. A jagged line of scary-ass pit bulls— five, no six—barking their massive heads off, snapping their steel-trap jaws and spewing foam.

Holy shit!

"Hush!" Miri is yelling. "Hush now!"

Yeah, right, Fen's thinking, but—*damn*—the barking just stops. The world goes vividly silent.

"Down," Miri commands, and again the dogs are obeying, every single one. Six thickly muscled bodies dropping to the ground, bellies flat to the earth. Clipped triangle ears, way too small for their giant heads, all pointed straight up to the sky. Beady eyes watching Miri's every move.

"Sorry!" Miri is turning to him, a pained look on her face. "I'm so sorry! I totally spaced about the dogs. I should've warned you! I'm sorry!"

"It's okay," he says, surprised at how *okay* he actually sounds. "Guess they're chained up, huh?" Because now that the noise isn't so mind-numbing, he realizes the dogs don't seem to be going anywhere. He sees the studded leather collars, the thick links of chain that appear to be bolted into earth.

"Yeah, they can't get to you. Unless you're within a couple of feet. Mostly it's to scare people."

"Well, it worked."

Fen gets a chuckle out of Miri for that, though her pained expression doesn't change.

"Really, it's okay, it's fine." He steps forward, pushes some hair out of her face, tucks it behind one ear. "I'm guessing the hellhounds must be part of the whole *End of the World as We Know It* plan?" She gives a wry smile, nods. "Some advice, though. If you're dealing with *zombies*, you might not want to keep the dogs on chains."

Another chuckle. "Noted," she says.

Together they head toward the house, thankfully not getting too close to the hellhounds, though the dogs *are* totally ignoring him now. Fen follows Miri up some stairs—tall ones leading to a big deck jutting out over the yard.

"Great view," Fen says, glancing back down at everything, taking in the large garden with its neat rows, the chicken coop with black and white and tan chickens wandering freely, pecking in the dirt and grass. At first he's confused by the stuff draped over the top of all the outbuildings—some kind of netting, black and tan and green. But then he understands.

Camouflage, that's what it is. Fen blinks a couple of times to be sure, but yeah, the whole place is camouflaged like something out of a war-zone movie.

"Welcome to Paradise," Miri says, and the irony's pretty obvious.

MIRI

Poe made even more bread before he left; at least there's something normal, warm and inviting, about her home.

"Smells really good in here," Fen comments as she nervously gives a quick tour through the living room, dining room, kitchen—all open-plan, so it doesn't take long. She wishes she could hit rewind, start over.

What was she thinking? How'd she totally space prepping the hellhounds (good one), totally space giving Fen some kind of heads-up?

Nerves, that's what it was. She'd been anxious all day, worrying about whether or not it was a good idea to actually bring Fen up here, worrying about Clay as well.

Miri had stopped by Clay's trailer on her way to school. She wanted to go ahead and break the news that she was planning on bringing Fen up here. Wanted to explain how she believed deep down that Clay and Fen would get along—*if* they met in a normal way, not at opposite ends of a gun. But Clay wasn't there—probably patrolling—so she'd had to leave a note.

"Poe makes his own bread," she tells Fen now. "He always makes a ton of food for me before he goes away. Like he thinks I'll starve to death."

"Wow. The only thing *my* dad does before he takes off is make sure the freezer is stocked with frozen dinners!"

Miri scoots to the fridge, opens the freezer door wide enough for Fen to see. "Poe does the same thing."

"Yeah, but those are homemade frozen dinners, I'm guessing." Fen nods to the perfectly stacked Tupperware containers. "My freezer's full of Lean Cuisine and Stouffer's."

"Try this," Miri says, cutting up a few slices of the loaf Poe left wrapped in a dish towel. It's no longer warm, but it's fresh. She lays the slices out on a plate, then she turns to the fridge again. "And you have to try the butter. June churns it herself."

"Of course she does. How long does *that* take?"

"Forever! Sometimes I go over and help her, but I haven't been for a while." Miri spreads the butter on thick. She slides the plate across the island counter, waits for Fen's reaction.

"I swear—this is the best bread and butter I've ever tasted. Hands down."

"Eat all you want," Miri tells him. "Then I'll show you the garden, and then we'll go out and check for eggs. That's what I usually do when I get home."

"Yeah, I was wondering about those chickens. How they were just . . . walking around?"

"Free-range, that's what it's called," Miri explains. "Better for the chickens, better for us because the eggs have a lot more nutrients when the hens get to eat different things."

"But . . . don't they ever wander over into the front yard? Like, even chained up, I bet the hellhounds could gobble them down pretty quick."

"Nope." Miri gives a firm shake of the head. "Dogs that kill chickens . . ." She raises the knife, pretends to slit her own throat. "They don't last very long around here."

Fen stops chewing, looks at her. "Seriously?"

"It's just . . ."

Oh shit. Those eyes! Suddenly Fen has the biggest, saddest puppy-dog eyes ever.

"It's just . . ." How to put this gently? "Once a dog starts killing chickens . . . they get a taste for it, and then they usually don't stop. So . . . you have to get rid of them . . . one way or another."

"So . . . you *kill* them?" Gulping, his puppy-dog eyes so very wide.

"Honestly, we haven't had to do that in a really long time!" she tells him. "And the hellhounds are *really* well trained."

Fen has put his half-eaten piece of bread back on the plate, staring at it.

Great! Now it'll be lodged in his brain forever—the image of Miri slitting a chicken-killing dog's throat.

Maybe it was a mistake bringing him up here, maybe they should've just stayed at his house or gone on a hike like usual. What if she lets it slip that she chops the heads off chickens when they need one for supper?

"You don't have to just eat bread, you know!" Way too bright and cheerful, but needing to distract Fen. "The fridge is full. Lots of snacks. Cheese—homemade, of course, thanks to June. Some ham Cyrus cured himself." Her thoughts dart to the pigs the old couple raise, how cute they are as piglets, how not-so-cute by butcher time. "We could even go out to the garden and pick some vegetables. Or strawberries! I'm pretty sure I saw some ripe strawberries yesterday."

"That's okay," he says—a half-hearted smile. "Maybe later. Bread really filled me up. Thanks."

"Sure." She wipes the crumbs from the counter, wraps the rest of the loaf back in the dish towel. "Hey, you brought your laptop, right?" Time for a total subject change. "How 'bout we listen to your soundscapes now?"

"I don't know . . ." Fen is hesitating. "Don't you want to show me around some more?"

She firmly shakes her head. She needs to block out all the weirdness she—and this whole place—are oozing. "I really want to hear your soundscapes." She reaches and takes both his hands across the counter. "Please?"

FEN

He can tell she's confused by the headphones.

"Speaker's not that great on the laptop," he explains. "Better to use these." And he's not lying . . . exactly. He *does* use the headphones when he's mixing, but it's mainly because he doesn't want anybody, like his mom or dad, to hear. He can't believe he's about to let Miri listen. Part of him wants to stall . . . indefinitely; part of him can't wait to know what she thinks.

"Okay . . . not sure what I should start you off with." He's got the laptop balanced on his knees, Miri right beside him on the large, soft couch in her sunny living room—one whole wall of windows. "Maybe something kinda recent." He scrolls through the folders, clicking on Detroit/Day, scrolling again till he gets to Detroit/Day #18.

"Wow, you've made a lot," she comments, voice overloud because of the headphones. "That's great!"

"You sure about this?" he asks, giving her one more chance to back out. "You ready?" he asks, though what he's really thinking is: *Am I ready?*

Miri gives a thumbs-up, so he takes a deep breath—it's now or never—and hits play.

Car horns—that's how Detroit/Day #18 starts out—a blast of car horns, and Miri's eyes go wide. Maybe he should've started with something softer, but it's too late now. He adjusts the sound level slightly, and leans back, tries his best to relax. Tries *not* to stare at Miri's face, tries *not* to watch for any minute or not-so-minute signs of puzzlement or confusion or, worse, boredom.

Instead he does a slow scan of the room, taking in his surroundings more fully now that he has time. There's a big wood-burning stove in one corner, logs stacked neatly beside it; a wooden rocking chair and a couple of end tables that all look handmade. Shelving beside the stove holds carved wooden bowls, old-fashioned-looking glass bottles, skulls—yep, skulls. Bleached white and gleaming. One's a cow—that's pretty obvious. But he's not sure about the others. Groundhogs maybe? *Haha, good one!* Fox? Raccoon? Squirrel? Animals he's seen scampering around the woods. Possibly a bird or two?

There are rocks as well—big ones, little ones; a couple of small metal baskets filled with rocks.

Kentucky is karst country.

He says it fast inside his head. He'd like to record Miri saying it—*if* she doesn't mind, doesn't think *that's* too . . . strange.

To the right of the couch, the wall is like a mini library—floor-to-ceiling books. Hardcovers, mostly, early editions by the looks of it. Didn't Miri say Poe collected old books? Fen's dad likes to read too, but mainly John Grisham thrillers, dog-eared paperbacks he buys mostly at yard sales. His mom falls asleep with a Kindle, but he honestly has no idea if she reads or just watches shows.

"Hey! Wait, that's it?" Miri cries out—voice overloud again. She slides one headphone up over her ear. "It's really cool, but I wanted it to be longer!"

He studies her a moment. Is she being serious?

"Yeah, I tend to keep them short and sweet—four to five minutes," he tells her. "Song length, basically. Though a few are longer, like twelve or fifteen. You can always loop the track so it keeps repeating. That's what you'd do with an art installation—not that what I do is *art*, I'm not saying that. I'm just playing around right now, but maybe someday . . ." He lets the words drift. Probably best if he stops talking.

"I want to hear more," she says, and she sounds (and looks) sincere, so he scrolls down the list again, clicks onto Detroit/Day #9. This time he closes his eyes, leans in a little so he can hear a trickle of sound filtering out of the headphones, follow along.

There's that street corner where he caught a fire hydrant blasting out water and the kids screaming around it. The basketball court with all the balls bouncing, shoes squeaking, snippets of trash talk. Next he goes to Detroit/Day #10, then Detroit/Day #11. He skips around a bit, goes to Detroit/Day #20, then Detroit/Day #60. After that he switches folders, clicks into Detroit/Night #2. The second time he'd snuck out at two a.m., not to meet anybody, not to get up to any "funny business," but to walk through the night alone, to record sounds. He'd ended up downtown, where he'd caught a homeless guy with a pack-a-day voice, muttering, "The world is jacked, man. The world is jacked." Over and over again. It was perfect. The thread that riffed through the whole soundscape, held it all together.

"The world *is* jacked," Miri echoes softly when he closes the laptop—enough for one day; he really doesn't want to bore her to death.

But she doesn't seem bored; she seems plugged in, amped up.

"This is really lame, but I've never even been to a city before. I've barely been out of the knobs." She turns to face him, tucking one leg under the other. "When I was growing up, Poe made it seem like this was the *only* place, that we didn't *need* anything or anybody else." She's obviously thinking through her words, choosing carefully. "Poe made it seem like it was the world *outside* Paradise that was . . . *jacked*, that we'd be better off here, that we'd always be safe." A pause. "But it's a lie." Her brows knit together. "Most of it anyway." She ducks her head so that her tangly hair curtains off her face. Before he can reach out and tuck some behind her ear, though—he loves doing that—she's done it herself, and she's lifted her chin and she's giving him a lopsided smile. "But forget about all that! It's not important. What *is* important is *this*." She taps a finger on the laptop. "Your soundscapes. They're beautiful. I want to hear every one. Every single one."

"Well, that might take a while," Fen jokes. "Days, weeks, months . . . even years," he adds, still making light of it—he doesn't really have soundscapes literally for *years*—but Miri suddenly gets serious.

"Days, weeks, months . . ." She's leaning in close, then closer, murmuring, her lips nearly touching his. "Years." Smiling into his smile because they're not really talking about soundscapes anymore; they're talking about something else, something more. "Years sounds pretty good to me."

"Yeah, I'm fine with years." Lips together, muffled words. "More than fine."

MIRI

The kissing is different—deeper, harder. Almost like they're angry with each other, but that's not it. They can't get close enough. That's the problem. Fen's mouth, his whole body, is pressed up against hers. And still, it's not close enough.

CLAY

It takes everything he has, every bit of strength inside him, just to stand there and not slam his fist through the wall. Or the window. Glass shattering. Shards flying. Blood splattering, probably. Blood everywhere. His blood; Bambi's blood. Maybe even Miri's blood.

Does he want that? Does he want to hurt Miri?

Clay turns away before he can test it—fist through glass, bloody knuckles wrapped around a tiny neck—he's seen that before. When he was little, of course. Some loser boyfriend of Cora's, totally cranked up, backhanding a glass on the coffee table in the trailer, then coming at his mom—fast, slamming her hard against the living room wall.

"I'm going to kill you, bitch."

But Cora wasn't easy to kill.

"Nine lives, baby," she always bragged. "Just like a kitty cat."

Cora had managed to reach the knife she always kept in her boot. A blink later and she'd already positioned it right below the ribs. The guy didn't even feel it, he was so high, but he did see the blood spurting out of his own body—his fist, his side—and freaked. Started backing up, slinking away. Trailing a bright red ribbon across the dirty linoleum, out the door, and down the rickety wooden steps.

Clay is not trailing blood, but something essential is leaking out of him as he silently moves off the porch and past the dogs, who are attentive but still. Something is seeping out of Clay as he skirts the gravel that would crunch, alert Miri. Though maybe not, since she's got her whole mouth, her whole body sucked up against that Bambi asshole.

What does she see in him anyway? Why was *she* the one to lean in and kiss *him*? Clay thought he could wait the whole new-kid thing out, thought Miri would get bored with such an obvious asswipe. Yeah, he's followed them a few times after school; so what? He saw how Bambi nearly wussed out at going into the cave—*their* cave, his and Miri's, the one Clay'd shown her years ago.

Why is Miri pushing herself at Fen when all she did was laugh at Clay, pull away? Why is she throwing herself at this total stranger when Clay's been right here all along?

Clay crumples the note he'd found stuck to his door—*her* note. *Poe's gone! We need to talk!* Throws it to the ground. And then he slips back through the trees, into the woods, leaving a trail of something only he can feel and see.

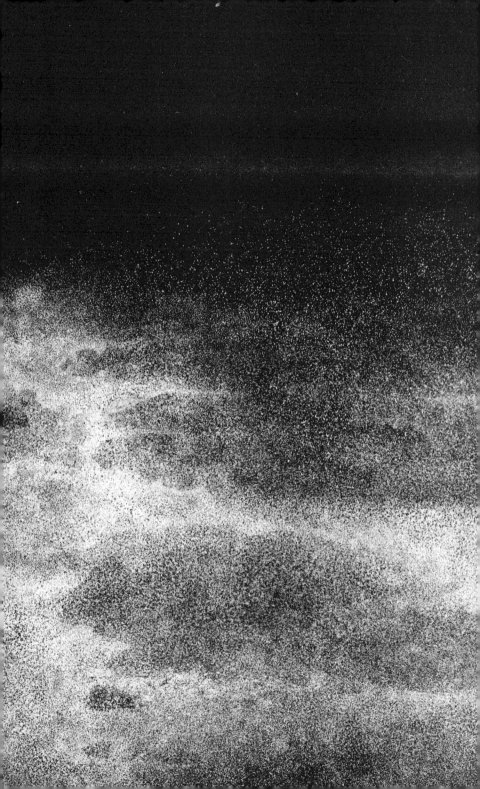

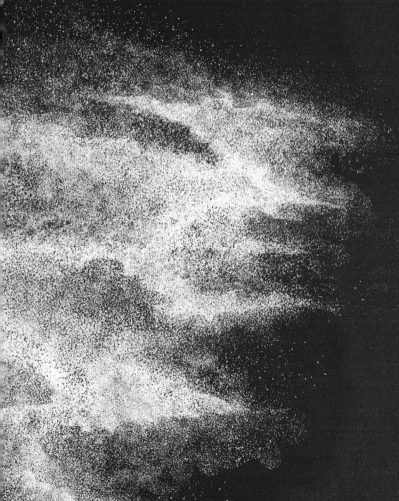

TWO

CLAY

Poe told him to check on the lab while he's gone. Which surprised Clay. He's never been inside the lab before, Poe's never let him—it's never been part of Clay's job description. He's always assumed Poe's been protecting him as much as he can. Keeping him from the nitty-gritty of the business since Clay was exposed from such an early age.

"Just take a look inside," Poe had said, handing over the key. "Make sure nothing seems like it's been disturbed." Eyes shifting to laser mode. "I don't have to tell you, son, not to touch anything."

"No, sir."

In the old days, Cora's lab was mainly the bathroom in the trailer, but really it was anywhere his mom could shake and bake without getting caught. The banged-up Ford Taurus worked just as well as anyplace. Plus she was mobile then, could deliver all through the knobs.

Crystal Cora. And her shit was pure—more than one tweaker's told him over the years—even if it was one-pot.

Poe's operation is definitely not one-pot. When Clay gets the door open, flips the switch, the whole place lights up, fluorescents lining the ceiling. Holy shit! Long stainless-steel tables, like maybe you'd see on TV. Fancy medical lab, scientists searching for the cure to cancer. Glass beakers, glass tubing—all of it clean, sparkling. The whole place neat as a pin, supplies stacked perfectly. Nothing like Cora's mini mountains of plastic Coke or Mountain Dew two-liter bottles, nine-volt batteries, crushed Sudafed boxes, coffee filters, empty containers of Drano.

Clay reaches out to touch a bright yellow suit hanging from a hook on the wall. Rubbery, protective. Two of them: big and little. His and hers, he guesses. Poe and Angel. A couple of gas masks hanging there too, bug-eyed, out of this world. Bright yellow gloves tucked into the straps.

Cora would put a bandana over her face—if she remembered—and that was it. She'd tell Clay to play outside in the woods if they were at the trailer, or she'd drive to a playground and lock him out of the car even when he got tired of the jungle gym or the swings. Even when it was raining or snowing, cold as freezer burn.

"Hey, son, all good?"

Poe's voice. Rumbling out of the fancy handheld. A little freaky how he knew exactly when to call. Clay glances up to the corners of the room, but he doesn't see any surveillance cameras.

"You in the lab?" Poe is asking. "Anything look disturbed to you?"

"No, sir," Clay answers. "It all looks good to me."

"Great." A muffled voice in the background—Angel, most likely.

"Okay, well, go ahead and lock it down. And make sure and remind Miri to check in before she goes to bed. That's what I told her to do."

"Yes, sir."

"Great. Thanks, son. Thanks for keeping an eye on things. Over and out."

"Over and out," Clay echoes, clicking off the handheld. He takes one more walk around the room. He's about to flip the lights when he sees a row of flat metal drawers nearby. For some reason he gets an irresistible urge to open one of the drawers, and so he does.

Tiny plastic baggies. The kind he grew up seeing, the kind he grew up getting his hands smacked away from.

Don't touch that, big calf!

Hundreds of tiny plastic baggies. Chunks of crystal stuffed inside—clear as rock candy.

He goes ahead and closes the drawer, flips the lights off. But not before he has taken a baggie—just one—fingers sliding it into his pocket, body turning and heading out the door.

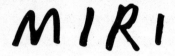

MIRI

"This is the bike I'm building. Or *re*building. It's an old Harley Pan-head."

They'd decided to skip school again, ditch the shit hole—too much of a temptation with Poe gone. First thing in the morning, she'd looped down the knob to pluck Fen from his house (after his dad had left), bring him back up to Paradise. They'd gathered the fresh eggs from the chicken coop—Fen loved that the eggs were still warm in the nesting boxes. Then she'd fixed him an omelet—she's never really mastered her favorite eggs Benedict. They'd eaten a bunch more bread with June's butter and with the strawberry jam Miri had canned herself last summer. There was a fair amount of kissing—a little sticky because of the jam.

Now they're in the garage, standing over Miri's framing table. Fen showed her something important, personal, yesterday—his soundscapes; she's decided to do the same.

"So . . . I'm mainly into old-school bikes. Vintage. Harley

produced the Panhead early on, like right at the end of World War Two. The name comes from this." Drumming her fingers over the silver rocker covers. "Because they resemble upside-down baking pans."

"Okay, yeah, I can see that." Fen nods.

"My favorite thing is this cool wishbone frame from a 1948 model," she continues. "And *my* Pan's got this bowlegged tubing and a triangle motor mount." Touching each part as she goes. "The engine's a two-cylinder, four-valve V-twin. Oh, and I'm gonna use an original leather solo seat—kinda like an old bicycle seat from way back when." Taking it all in for a moment. "The bike's a mutt, basically, if you stop to think about it." Laughing at that.

"Where do you get the different parts?" Fen asks.

"Sometimes we already have old bikes lying around, and we cannibalize one and use it for something else. But lots of times we order parts online, or Poe will find something vintage when he's on the road—like this trip he's taking. Who knows what he'll come back with?"

"Reminds me of a skeleton or something, the way it's all laid out on the table."

"Exactly!" Miri gives him an approving nod. "You start with a skeleton, the bones of the bike, and then build up from there." Grabbing onto one of the swing arms. "This might sound weird, but sometimes I think it's why my favorite book is *Frankenstein*. Because I relate, you know?" Checking in with Fen, making sure he's following, or at least trying to—and he is. "With a bike, I'm always building something new out of old parts, different pieces, and I'm never totally sure if it's all going to work in the end. If this new creation will be awesome, or a dud . . . basically a monster."

"It's the same with my soundscapes!" Fen tells her. "Sometimes I'm really excited about a new project, and I think all these random sounds I've recorded will fit perfectly together, but they don't. They just sound . . . wrong."

"Yeah." She nods. "Same here." They're eyeing each other, and Miri has the nearly overwhelming urge to tug Fen close, mash her lips to his like they've been doing a lot of lately, but she also just wants to stand here and bask in this *thing* happening between them, this connection. She's never really felt exactly *this* before, not even with Clay, who is closer to her than anybody.

"What we do," Miri begins—is it stupid to try to put it into words? "You and me, it's honestly not that different. Your soundscapes and my bikes . . ."

"We both build something new out of something old," he finishes for her.

"Yeah." She raises one eyebrow—not super successfully. "I guess we've both got a little Dr. Frankenstein in us."

Fen puts both arms out straight and stiff, does a pretty bad Frankenstein monster imitation, which cracks them both up.

"Seriously, though." Fen sobers. "This is probably a really stupid question . . ."

"'There are no stupid questions!' At least that's what Poe always says."

"I think every grown-up says that, and I don't think it's true. I think people ask really, really stupid questions sometimes."

"Example: the buzzards," Miri inserts, and Fen agrees.

"But *my* stupid question of the day . . ." He pauses, formulating.

"I know you build this bike from the bones up, put it all together, but *how* do you put it all together? I'm guessing you don't use superglue."

Miri cocks her head, grins. "I'll show you." And then she goes to grab her welding gear.

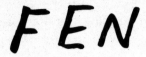

FEN

The sound is deafening, even with the squishy green earplugs Miri gave him. And the metal helmet is heavy, the visor so dark, it's like he's back inside the cave before his eyes had adjusted.

"It's a MIG welder," Miri had explained as she rolled a big silver machine on wheels over to the framing table. "M-I-G." Spelling it out for him. "Metal Inert Gas, as opposed to a T-I-G welder. Tungsten Inert Gas."

"Right," Fen had said, nodding, as if he'd understood anything she'd just said.

Now sparks are flying—he can see *that* through the murk. Kind of like a mini Fourth of July celebration. But he doesn't understand how Miri's "checking the joints she's already done" as she said, how she can work with so much bulk—the helmet, the visor, the thick leather gloves and apron. He's one giant sweat ball under it all, and he's not even doing anything, just standing there.

"Keep the visor down until I tell you," she'd warned before the earsplitting roar took over everything. "You can burn out your retinas if you look directly at the light."

So, yeah. In theory, he and Miri are the same, just like she said, making something new out of something old, making something beautiful or possibly something monstrous. But in reality, what Miri does is a whole lot *harder*—he sees that now. Welding is on a completely different level than playing around with sound. Fen sits on his bed with his laptop and headphones, mixing tracks together, while Miri actually works with fire and molten metal—things that could kill you or at least blind and/or scar you for life.

Which leaves Fen to wonder. What does Miri—who's a total *badass* in basically every way—see in him, a geeky sound nerd? Fen's not sure, but he just prays she keeps seeing it.

The fireworks have gotten bigger—giant exploding stars in a night sky. Fen takes a step forward, and through the murk he can make out red-hot lines of lava, fine strands of it, like Miri is stitching her monster's body together, sewing with fire instead of thread.

Fen's just starting to think about how he might capture the essence of Miri welding. Not the ground-shaking drone of the MIG, that would be too much, but the sound of fire itself, of metal bones being joined together. But then the spark snuffs out—a giant birthday candle blown to black—and Miri's flipping switches, levers. The silence is shocking, just like when the hellhounds stopped their barking.

"Knock, knock, anybody home?"

Miri is rapping her knuckles against the glass visor, then she's helping him lift the bulky helmet off his head. The air seems so much cooler now, like he's stepped out of a sauna. Sweat is streaming down his face and neck, his hair wet and matted to his skull, T-shirt soaked through when he removes the heavy apron. He's a mess, but it's okay. Miri's a mess too.

"Here you go." She grabs a couple of faded towels from a hook on the wall and hands one over. "Gets pretty hot in here with the MIG running and all that body armor." She's swiping at her own face with the other towel, but she keeps missing a couple of dark splotches, so Fen tries to help. The spots are stubborn, oily, though.

"Grease monkey." Miri sticks her chin out to make it easier for him. "That's what Poe used to call me. His little grease monkey."

"Grease monkey," he murmurs as he moves in closer, kissing her, dirt and all—no way to resist.

CLAY

He's listened to their voices all day. Not what they're saying. He won't get that close. But he can hear the rise and fall of their laughter—so much laughter. He can picture exactly how Miri's nose wrinkles up when she's really losing it, exactly how she'll start gasping for air—mouth open, eyes wide like a fish after it's been caught and he's holding it in his hands, checking to see if it's worth keeping or throwing back.

Of course they're skipping school together—Clay's not surprised. Though it did make him want to punch something (or someone) when he realized how she'd buzzed down the knob at the regular school time but then come right back up, Bambi in tow.

Dude can't even drive his own damn self up the knob—fancy truck and everything? Clay's scoped out the Ram, of course. Thought about knifing a tire deep in the night, but controlled the urge. All that would do would bring Miri running to the rescue.

Clay keeps patrolling like Poe asked him to do, but he goes

higher up to avoid Miri's and Bambi's voices. He circles the lab a few times, then winds his way to the top of Paradise, and stands at the edge of the overlook, gazing down, thinking how from this distance the knobs are like rumples in a giant unmade bed.

Clay stays at the top of the knob all day, till the sun starts going down, hoping Bambi will be gone, but he's not. In fact, the voices grow even louder as he sits on his trailer steps in the dusk.

What is it about noises traveling farther as the dark's settling in? He knows this from a lifetime spent in the woods, tracking, hunting. But he's also had it confirmed for him in a book somewhere.

Poe used to give him books, especially right after he dropped out of school.

"School's not for everybody," he'd told Clay, trying to make him feel better. "Lots of folks were self-taught in the old days. You can learn a lot from reading a few good books."

Clay likes some of the "good books" Poe's given him more than others. He finished *The Last of the Mohicans* in no time, but he's never been able to get past the first couple of pages of *Moby Dick*.

Bambi's probably read a lot of "good books." He definitely has "nerd" written all over him. Maybe that's what Miri likes about him, and maybe Clay understands a little—if he stops to think about it clearly. But nothing's clear when the image of Miri pops back into his brain. The image of her kissing Bambi first, pushing her whole self into him.

Clay shakes his head—slow, steady. He wants to get it out of his head—not just the image of Miri on the couch, but the sound of her laughing, the sound of her loving somebody else.

FEN

They probably need to get him home—it's past dark, his dad will wonder why his truck's there but he's not—and yet neither of them are making a move.

Basically, they've been wrapped around each other—possibly for hours. Lying on a blanket on the ground beside a bubbling spring (great sound!). A place they'd come to cool off after Miri'd put away the MIG.

"Did you know that cicadas start chirping louder when it gets hotter?" Miri's voice is hoarse from not talking for so long. "They get faster, too. More chirps per minute. One cicada can end up louder than a chain saw."

"Cicada . . ." His brain is fuzzy, voice garbly like hers. "That's a bug, right?"

"Okay, Mr. Sound Guy." Laughing, rolling away—not too far, but still. The cold weasels in—especially the parts of him that are still damp from sun and sweat and where Miri's body was pressed tight to his. "That's what we've been listening to this whole time."

Huh. Not what *he's* been listening to; he's been totally oblivious to anything but Miri.

"Seriously?" She shifts up onto one elbow to peer down at him in the dimming light. "That chain saw buzzing. All around? The constant droning? You haven't noticed it?"

"Not with you here," he admits—super corny, but true. She rolls her eyes, but she leans in to kiss him.

"Don't they have cicadas in Detroit?" she asks after a moment, clearly curious.

"Not sure, honestly." Pausing, listening for real this time. "I guess there's so much other noise in the city, maybe they're there, but you just don't notice them so much?"

"Well, it's hard *not* to notice them here. Especially late in the summer. It gets pretty intense sometimes. Like I said, cicadas get louder with heat."

Fen reaches for his phone lying beside him on the blanket, barely glances as he hits record. Miri lies back, but stays close so that their arms are touching, shoulder to wrist, melded together. A flash to when she was welding earlier, joining silver bones together.

"Could you live off cicadas when the shit hits the fan?" he ponders out loud after he's hit stop on his phone. "Do they taste like apples too?"

"Asparagus." Said in all seriousness. "That's what they taste like. And you can eat cicadas raw or roast them." A pause. "Actually, they're not bad in a salad. Crunchy, like croutons."

"No thanks!" He's shaking his head. "No way I'm putting bugs in my salad!"

"Clearly you're not ready for TEOTWAWKI."

"TEO . . ." Trying to repeat after Miri, but failing.

"The End of the World as We Know It." Helping him out. "TEOTWAWKI."

"Right."

Miri gets up first and pulls him to standing, then they both lean down to fold the blanket, grab the basket of snacks they'd brought—not stink bugs or cicadas! Just more bread and some cheese and ham, a few strawberries from the garden.

It's not just the fireflies—"lightning bugs," as Miri calls them—lining the path back to the house, but a string of twinkly Christmas lights.

"Angel's touch," Miri explains, and it takes him a minute to realize she's talking about an actual person. "Angel's my dad's girlfriend." By the slight change in tone, Fen can tell that Angel's not Miri's favorite person. "Does *your* dad have a girlfriend?"

"He's had a couple on and off since the divorce." Shrugging, then making a decision. "Dad's an alcoholic," Fen says, not for sympathy, just stating a fact. "I mean, he *was*. He's been sober awhile now, which is awesome, by the way. But he's a workaholic, too. So . . . I guess all of that has gotten in the way of any serious relationship after my mom."

"Sounds rough." Miri leans into him as they're walking.

"Not really. It's fine now. Living with him . . ." Fen shrugs. "It's working out. In all honesty, I think my mom wanted a break. I don't blame her. Being a single mom is hard."

"I guess Poe's always been a single dad," Miri says. "My mom died when I was almost three."

"I'm so sorry." He holds tight to her hand. "*That* must've been awful."

"Not really. I mean, I don't remember her at all. So it's not as hard as maybe it would be if I *did* remember her." Glancing at him. "Do you think that's weird?"

"No. Not at all! You were only *three*. I don't think I remember anything from when I was three."

"And it's not like I have many photos to look at," Miri says, more to herself. "Actually, there's only one."

"What do you mean?" Staring at her. "None of you together? Like, when you were a baby? Don't you have a baby book, or a family album, or something like that?"

"Nada. Zip." Miri shrugs. "Poe always said we didn't need that stuff, that it wasn't important. When he moved us here, he just left everything behind, walked away. Any photos, or whatever, probably just got dumped in the trash—who knows?"

"Wow, that's . . ." Fen's trying to find the right word. "Harsh."

Miri shrugs again. "That's Poe."

They put the blanket and uneaten snacks away. Then head for the bike. (It's crazy how the hellhounds don't even look his way anymore.)

"Hey, what's the plan for tomorrow?" Fen asks before Miri kick-starts the engine. "Poe gets back Saturday, right?"

"Pretty sure. I'll double-check. Clay will know." She glances quickly—nervously?—past his shoulder, out toward the trees.

"So, Clay's around?" Turning to follow her gaze, half expecting a scary jump cut like in a horror movie—Clay suddenly appearing out of the woods like Jason in *Halloween*.

"Haven't seen him lately, but he's around."

Fen watches the dark trees a little while longer. Sometimes it *does* feel like he's being watched here, in these woods.

"Should we skip again?" Miri's asking. "Think it's worth the risk?"

"Oh yeah." Fen turns back to give her his full attention. "Definitely."

CLAY

He's always known about the parties. He's just never been tempted before. Not till Miri's and Bambi's voices pushed him off his porch steps, off Paradise, onto the road in his Ford 4 × 4, over to the next knob over. Hanging out with Trent and Stevie, two asswipes who used to make fun of him at school. Looking at him now like he's made of gold.

"No shit, Clay, you holding?"

Just a tilt of the head and that's all it takes. He is new in their eyes, and they would follow him anywhere.

And they do, back to his truck, where he runs a hand across the hood, brushing any dirt or rust away. And then he's taking the baggie out of his pocket and emptying half of it, a mini mountain of bluish white, just enough moonlight to see the quality.

"Whoa, that's Wizard batch."

"I work with him now," Clay says, and he can feel the change, the guys looking at him, seeing him like someone new.

"No way! You cooking for him?"

"He's teaching me." Not a complete lie, right? Poe's got him doing the security guard thing, and now—trusting him enough to check his lab. It's not a far stretch to sharing the recipe, showing him how to batch.

"Well, what are we waiting for? That shit's going to blow away on the next damn breeze." Trent's already got his wallet out, tugging his license from the folds. He leans forward, but then says, "Sorry, dude," and shoves it toward Clay before Clay can say no, before he can explain that he's never tried it before. But his hands are already taking the plastic rectangle, flattening out the mini mountain of crystal, cutting it into lines. Second nature. A lifetime of watching Cora, her bony fingers, her swift hands.

Be generous and give them more. The first time at least. Keeps 'em coming back.

Cora's words from long ago.

Does Clay want them coming back? The half packet in his pocket won't be shit when they think they have a new supply line. What will he do then? How long will Poe be gone? Bigger question—how long will it take him to notice what's missing?

"Fuckin' right!" Trent sniffs hard at the rolled tube of a five-dollar bill, practically sucking on it, not wanting to miss a speck. Handing it over to Stevie, who starts whooping like an idiot once he's got a nose full.

Clay had planned to smudge the third line once Trent and Stevie were high and satisfied, dust it to nothing in the dark, but they're both staring at him, pupils big and black like crows' eyes. Like watching him will be an extra hit.

"What you waiting for?" Trent says, and Clay is already cringing at the next word. *Retard*. What Trent used to call him at school. *Hey there, retard, what you waiting for?*

But the "retard" doesn't come.

"Yo, Clay, it's your turn!"

Clay takes the rolled-up bill Trent hands him and leans in over the hood of the truck, leans in close to the line of crank glowing in the moonlight, and fulfills what surely was his destiny from the very beginning. Cora's son after all.

MIRI

She's totally wired when she gets back from taking Fen home—she'd stopped at Clay's, but his truck was gone—so she decides to do some work on the Panhead before going to bed.

Inside the garage, she rolls the MIG over to the framing table, but she doesn't suit up just yet. She scans the silver bones, the body emerging. She loves the vintage wishbone frame, loves how it will fit her body perfectly—one of the reasons to build your own bike. She should've explained that to Fen; she can tomorrow. Bikes off the assembly line are always too big—even the ones marketed to women.

When the Panhead's done, it won't have any extra bulk; it'll be light, with a small engine, smallish fuel tank—no room to carry extra gas. She remembers how she scolded Fen that first day, but it's different when you're working with two wheels instead of four. Just because you can't bring a spare of anything doesn't mean you can't be prepared, make sure you stop when you need to, make sure you've mapped out your route.

The day she turns eighteen—that's when she'll take off, and Poe won't be able to stop her. Legally, she'll be an adult—nothing he can do. The plan is to head out west, like she's told Clay. New Mexico, Arizona, Nevada—not sure which one, but maybe she'll give them each a try. She's read that there are still a few desert races, some in the Mojave, but she has to do more research.

Would Fen come out west with her? He's a few months older, they'll graduate together—if he even stays at the shit hole. But maybe he won't; maybe his dad will decide to move again, or Fen will want to go back to Detroit to live with his mom.

Probably Fen's planning on college, something Miri hasn't even considered. She's just always assumed she'd find a job in a garage fixing bikes and/or cars wherever she ends up. She knows she's got the skills to make enough money to get by. What does she need college for? But Fen's got "college boy" written all over him. Maybe he could find a college somewhere out west; maybe they could even get an apartment together.

Okay, wow! Getting a little ahead of herself, right? Here she is, planning some kind of bright and shiny future with Fen when she has no idea how he really feels about her, how he *will* feel about her once she tells him about Poe. Because she's gonna have to tell him. Sooner or later. And it needs to be sooner. Before the buzzards, or someone else in town, does it for her.

"Hey, Fen, just letting you know, my dad cooks meth for a living."

Miri tries it out—voice echoing in the empty garage.

"Yeah, and that girlfriend I mentioned? Angel? She's his partner. They cook meth together in a hidden lab not that far from the house. Oh, and Clay's involved too. But just a little bit."

What's a "little bit" anyway? *Miri* doesn't even know. She's kept her eyes shut, ears blocked, acted like she doesn't understand what's going on.

Accessory.

The word pops into her head. And she has to ask herself: What would she say to Fen—to the police or a judge, for that matter—if Poe got caught?

I didn't know.

Yeah, right.

What Fen—or anybody—would say.

I was blind.

No, not exactly, not for a while now.

I was stupid.

Okay, that's a start.

I was disappointed. I was scared.

Getting closer.

And anyway, now that Miri is talking to an imaginary Fen, imaginary judges or juries or whatever, she has to ask herself: How is it that Poe *hasn't* gotten caught in all this time?

Clay's told Miri what he remembers about the raid on Cora, about the flashing lights and men with guns busting in and dragging his mom away in the middle of the night. Why hasn't that happened to Poe? Unless, of course, the black helicopters Poe keeps claiming to see are the prelude to that.

If Poe gets busted before Miri turns eighteen, she'll go straight into foster care—no family to take her. Maybe June and Cyrus—they're almost like grandparents—but would Miri really want that? All that end-of-the-world shit, *twenty-four seven*?

Maybe Fen's dad would take her! But is that realistic? A dad taking in his son's girlfriend because *her* dad's in prison? Not likely. Plus, Miri's never even met the guy. He might be as crazy as Poe, though she doubts it.

Miri grabs the helmet, the thick leather gloves and apron—getting herself ready. Poe taught her to weld when she was about nine, but she'd been watching him for much longer. Once she was able to use the torch herself, she'd practice running weld beads on a piece of scrap metal for hours at a time. It wasn't easy at first—it took a lot of hand-eye coordination, Poe explained, because you're looking at something through a thick plate of glass—a thick, *dark* plate of glass. But after a while she could stop and start the weld whenever she wanted, and the seams were smooth. Then she went on to practice the basic joints: butt joints, corner joints, tee joints.

Miri clicks the visor into place, flips the switch on the MIG. The sound is deafening, mind-numbing, and it's exactly what she needs.

CLAY

Maybe he's never seen stars before. Really seen them. Like he's seeing them now. So close he can almost touch them. So close he's part of them, floating inside the specks of light, bits of warmth. Not cold like he remembers learning about in school. Stars are cold, that's what some teacher said, right? Cold and dead and distant. But what did that teacher know—because what Clay feels now is warmth, flooding through him, and he knows it's the star glow that's making him feel this way.

Same with the meth. Rock. Crystal. Sometimes meth is called ice. But other times it's called fire. And he can see why now, can feel both working inside him. Ice making him clear—clearer than he's ever been. Like a fog lifting from his brain. So many thoughts zinging straight and true, none of them tangled like usual.

"I want to go back to school," he announced not long after the first line.

"What the hell?" Trent said. "What you talking about?"

"I want to take all those tests I failed," Clay explained. "I want to show those asswipes I can do it."

"You want to ruin a perfectly good high by going back to school?" Stevie cried, and then he started laughing and couldn't stop.

"Retard," Trent said. "You are one crazy, motherfuckin' retard."

And it didn't bother Clay this time. Being called a retard by Trent. He loved Trent now. Loved him like the brother he'd never had. Loved Stevie, too, though maybe a little less. Just because Stevie's laugh was so annoying, kind of like a donkey.

"You're hilarious, retard. I never knew." Trent puts his arm around Clay's shoulders, or at least tries. Trent is a shrimp next to Clay; how had he never seen that before? Or maybe he had, and just ignored it. Everybody's pretty much a shrimp next to Clay, but that doesn't matter because he always felt small. Back there in school. He always felt small even though he was a giant, a big calf. Because of who he was, who his mom was, where they lived—a broken-down single-wide halfway up the knob. He sees it all so clearly now, and instead of turning away, he wants to fix it.

"I want to go back to school and pass all those stupid tests," Clay says, and he starts to move away, but Trent hangs on.

"School's out forever for us, dude," Trent says. "Time to party."

And that's just what they do. They pile into Clay's truck and head over to the next knob. Preacher's Knob, it's called, which is right because Clay is in the process of seeing the light, of being saved. All these years he lived in the darkness but had the light in his grasp. Literally, sometimes. His chubby toddler hands reaching for the sparkly crystal, piled on the kitchen table or else stuffed inside tiny plastic squares.

"Don't touch!" Cora would scream, slapping his hand. Smacking his face for good measure. "How many times I got to tell you, never touch Mommy's shit!"

It's not Mommy's shit running through his body right now, of course. It's Poe's, but the recipe is nearly the same, he knows that for a fact. Angel spent time with Cora before Cora got sent up, before Poe moved here. Angel knew all Cora's secrets, her magic, and Clay is pretty sure though not positive that Angel shared those secrets in order to get in good with Poe. Angel wasn't there when the DEA raided Cora's trailer, otherwise she'd be up at KCIW serving fifteen to twenty too.

"Hey, this is what I call a party!" Trent is saying, after they've parked the truck on the side of the road behind a line of others, after they've wound through the woods and come to the clearing, a bonfire roaring. Too hot for a fire, but still, what else do you do around here when you've got a pile of sticks, some fast-food trash, and a Zippo?

Clay can make out shadows milling around the fire, maybe a dozen. Faceless from where he is, but some of the voices he knows from school, from town. Trent hands him something cold—a can of beer—and he downs it in one go, he's that thirsty.

"Damn," Trent says, and then Clay is given another.

"What's *he* doing here?" a voice asks. And in the old days, at school, Clay might've walked right up and punched the guy in the face, no warning. But tonight he's happy to just stand where he is, sip the beer, let the shadows be.

"He's working for the Wizard," Trent says.

"Yeah, handyman kind of shit. Watchdog," somebody mumbles. "Hell, he's always done that."

"No, I mean, he's *working* for him now," Stevie clarifies.

There's a silence and Clay feels all eyes—even the ones way back from the fire, way back in the dark—fastening onto him.

"And it's better than the stories," Trent tells them. "*Way* better."

Something shifts, and the want, the need, coming off those shadows, it's almost too much for Clay to bear. Like the shadows are aliens and they've suddenly started sucking his life force through some kind of mind meld, like on TV or in the movies.

"I got money," a voice says.

"Yeah, me too."

"How much you selling?"

Clay starts to back up. The glow he's feeling inside is still good, but it's been sucked a little by all the shadows.

"He ain't selling nothing tonight," Trent says, seeming to sense what's going on as well. "Come back tomorrow night, and maybe we'll be here." Trent turns to Clay, leans in. "Right?"

Clay makes some kind of sideways motion with his head, but it's enough. The circle of shadows opens, and Clay finds himself moving right to the fire's edge.

MIRI

It's nearly three in the morning by the time she leaves the garage. Her T-shirt is soaked through and her arms are like jelly.

All she wants is to fall into bed—sweaty, dirty, doesn't matter. But as soon as she walks through the door, she hears a familiar *MEEP-MEEP-MEEPing*. Poe signaling her on the handheld—a good thing, since she wants to find out exactly when he's coming home.

"I've been trying you all night, where the hell you been?" Poe demands without even a hello.

"In the garage. Working on the Pan. Lost track of time."

"Have you talked to Clay tonight?"

Her heart quickens. "No, why?" Has Clay said something to Poe?

"He's not answering, and he needs to check in."

Pulse slowing. "I think he's just doing what you asked—*patrolling*." Using Poe's own word, throwing it back at him, but he doesn't seem to notice.

"You've seen him?" The reception isn't great, which surprises Miri. Poe always claims he could be in another country with his Black Ops handhelds, and they'd still be able to talk.

"Yeah," she answers, glad for the sudden rumble of static—a buffer for the lie. "He's around," she adds. Because even if Clay's staying hidden, even if she technically hasn't seen him, he's here. She knows it. Where else would he be?

"Want you to stop by the trailer in the morning, before school. Remind him that he needs to check in with me. More than once a day." Static takes over for a moment, but then the line goes clear. "Oh, and it's going to be longer than I thought. Couple more days. We'll be back Sunday."

Miri feels a weight lifting. "Sunday?"

"That's right. Sunday." Another flare of static. "You working on the garden?"

"Yeah." She'll get Fen to help her tomorrow.

"Good." Voices in the background. Angel maybe? But the voices sound deeper—guy voices. "Okay, I gotta go. Get that message to Clay." A pause. "How's the Pan coming anyway?"

"Great."

"Can't wait to see it up and running," Poe says, which is kinda weird. It's not like he's taken a lot of interest in bikes lately. He's hardly set foot in the garage in months. "Hey, Mir, I love you." Another surprise. When's the last time Poe's told her *that*? "And things are going to be different when I get back. You'll see. I love you, and—" A roar of static this time, and the line cuts out.

Miri stands there, staring at the handheld for a while. Weird. Maybe Poe was drunk—though he wasn't slurring. Maybe he was high, though he doesn't tweak, according to Clay, at least. She waits a few minutes to see if Poe will call back, finish his sentence, then she sets the handheld down, walks to the big front windows.

It's dark outside. She tries to see past her own reflection in the glass, but she can't. She knows if somebody—Clay—were out there in the night, they'd be able to watch her every move and she'd never even know.

FEN

He's never actually worked in a garden, but of course he gets the basic concept. Pull the weeds to make the rows neater, pick the vegetables and put them in a basket.

"Hey, I never knew asparagus grew this way," he says, snapping off one of the tiny green trees sticking straight up from the ground.

Miri gives him an amused look. "How else would asparagus grow?"

"Um . . . like corn or something? Wrapped in a husk?"

"City boy," she cracks. "You know, when we first met, I used to call you Detroit. Inside my head. Before I knew your name."

"I've lived other places," he informs her.

"Nah. You'll always be Detroit to me." She swats at some pesky gnats. One thing about gardening: it sure is buggy. And hot, and messy. They've got dirt caked into their knees, dirt streaked along their arms. Even on their faces from slapping at a bug or wiping away sweat.

"This is a lot of work," Fen admits after they've moved on to another row, and they're not even halfway through the whole thing yet. "I mean, I'm not complaining. *At all.* I'm just saying. It's a big-ass garden. Do you do this all on your own? Or does Poe help? Or . . . Angel?"

"Poe does the tilling, and we do the planting together, but once things are growing, it's basically on me," Miri says. "Clay helps a lot." Catching herself. "Usually." Glancing off to one side—into the woods.

It takes an effort *not* to follow her gaze.

"I think you'd like Clay," Miri says in a lower voice. Does *she* think he's out there too, listening, watching? Still, Fen doesn't turn. "I think you'd get along if . . ."

He wasn't using me for target practice?

Fen doesn't say it out loud, of course. "Yeah. We could hang out . . . sometime." Trying to sound enthusiastic. "That'd be great."

Slowly, they work down the rows of yellow squash and green zucchini, and Fen stops every once in a while to record something—chickens, mostly. The chickens keep wandering over to the edge of the garden, swiveling their heads like they're checking Fen and Miri out, making sure they're doing what they're supposed to be doing. And they keep up this nonstop chatter—Fen had no idea before hanging out at Miri's that chickens were so vocal. There's the usual clucking he's known about from kids' books or TV shows or whatever, but there's also this . . . keening, that's the word. One hen will start *keening* and then another will join in and then it's a whole chorus of keening chickens.

"Chorus of keening chickens. Say that three times fast!" he tells

Miri, and just like with the karst tongue twister, they get stuck and keep cracking up.

"What's the deal with that rooster over there?" Fen asks when they're taking a water break. "Never hear a peep out of him."

"You're out of luck," Miri says. "Big Red only crows at the crack of dawn."

"Big Red?"

"Not a very creative name," Miri admits. "But he's big . . ."

"And he's red," Fen finishes.

"Maybe you could be here when Big Red crows. Maybe you could . . ."

They exchange a look.

"Isn't Poe coming back tomorrow?" he asks, and she shakes her head.

"I talked to him last night. He's not getting back till Sunday."

Okay, he knows he's blushing—so stupid. Why does skin *do* that? Hopefully Miri will think it's the heat, the sun.

"Want me to stay the night?" he blurts, and—whoa!—that sounded wrong, crude. "I mean . . ." Backtracking. "I could stay here . . . on the couch or whatever . . . and then I'd be here . . . at the crack of dawn . . . to record Big Red."

Miri reaches out and puts her fingertips to his throat, right where his heartbeat is pulsing. "I wanted to do that the first day," she whispers. "We'd just met and you were embarrassed about running out of gas."

"That was pretty embarrassing," Fen admits.

"I want you to stay the night," she says, keeping her eyes glued to his. "I want you to stay here with me."

"I want that too." His heart does this crazy thump inside his chest. A whole night with Miri. A. Whole. Night.

"What about *your* dad?" A ripple of worry. "Won't it be hard to get away?"

Fen thinks it through. "I'll just tell Dad I've made a new friend, and I'm going to play some video games or something, and crash on the couch so I don't have to drive those roller-coaster roads late at night." Deciding. "I don't have to mention the fact that the friend's a girl instead of a guy."

Taking a breath. "Think that'll work?"

"Well, that could be Plan A," Fen says. "If it doesn't fly, I'll go to Plan B, and just . . . *sneak* out. Dad always shuts himself up in his room after dinner, and basically never comes out again. Honestly, sneaking out wouldn't be that hard."

"And I could come down and get you so the truck doesn't alert him," Miri throws in. "Meet you at the end of your driveway." She snaps her fingers. "And I could give you one of Poe's handhelds. Then you could let me know which plan we're going with."

"A handheld's like a walkie-talkie, right?"

"Roger that," Miri says, mock military.

"Okay, so we get to speak in code?" Turning little kid, he can't help it. "Like ten-four and all that?"

"Um . . . only if you want to?" Miri has one eyebrow raised.

"Hell yeah!" Giving a thumbs-up. "I mean, roger that."

Miri shakes her head. "Goofball," she teases, pushing him away, but instantly pulling him back again.

MIRI

Late in the afternoon, Miri runs Fen down the knob—after they'd had some fun with "walkie-talkies" and silly lingo. Better for Miri not to cross paths with Fen's dad. That would take too much explaining.

Back home again, Miri looks at the heaping baskets of cucumbers and asparagus, peas and spinach Fen had helped her lug into the screened-in porch. She dumps the spinach into the industrial sink to scrub the dirt off, pauses to put on some music, and pauses again.

Ever since Fen started tuning her in to the whole ambient sound thing, she finds that she can just sit and listen, appreciate all the sounds she's mainly taken for granted—or at least hasn't paid attention to for a while.

Like the quail calling from somewhere deep in the woods (quails like to stay hidden) with its clear, distinctive "Bob-*white!*" Or the Kentucky warbler with its string of extra-perky "Churree! Churree! Churree!" Or the multitude of sparrows, a constant in these woods, with their nonstop fluty trills. Or the mourning doves, a pair, of course, since they mate for life (Fen loved *that* when she told him, but he'd asked, "Why do they sound so sad, then?"). Or the mockingbirds, who steal all the songs just because they can.

Or even the bee buzzing at the screen door—a honeybee, Miri knows without glancing over. Because a wood bee, or a bumblebee, would have a much louder buzz.

Sound. It's so important to Fen, and the funny thing is, it's important to Clay, too.

Miri remembers all the times Clay has shushed her in the woods so they can listen for their rescued baby owl's call—*any* owl's call—a wild turkey's gobble, a coyote's lonesome cry. Clay loves listening to nature, and so does Fen. In fact, Clay could introduce Fen to stuff Miri doesn't even know about—sounds she's not even familiar with because she doesn't spend as much time alone in the deepest parts of the woods, like Clay does.

A few minutes later the spinach is clean and she starts chopping. The honeybee bumps against the screen and she glances at it, then beyond to the garden, and the woods, and lets out a sigh.

Clay's avoiding her. Pretty obvious at this point. She wishes he'd just come on over, like always, so they could talk like they used to, so she could explain about Fen. Though maybe that wouldn't be so easy. Explaining about Fen. It's not like she completely understands either, why she felt so connected to him almost from the moment they met.

It was love at first sight.

That's what Poe used to say about Miri's mom. Laura. When he used to talk about her. Before Angel.

Our eyes met across a crowded room, and that was it. I was a goner.

So maybe it's in her DNA—to see somebody and to instantly know you want to be with them. Maybe always.

Of course it didn't work out that way for Poe and her mom; it probably won't work out for Miri and Fen, either. Especially once she reveals the whole thing about the Wizard and what goes on up here in "Paradise."

"Shit!" The chopping knife Miri's using slips, a slice of red across her fingertip, a few crimson drops marring fresh green. "Shit!" She sucks at the blood, but the cut is stubborn despite its size. So she heads over to the sink, holds her hand under the cold running tap water.

Waiting for the bleeding to stop, watching the red swirl down the drain, she makes a decision. She'll tell Fen everything, but she'll wait until tomorrow. She doesn't want to spoil tonight.

FEN

In the end he doesn't even need the handheld lodged under the seat of his truck, but he's glad to have it, glad Miri showed him how to use it. They'll be able to talk every night when they're not together. Better than a sorry-ass cell phone.

"Really glad you've made a friend," his dad says, not even batting an eye at Fen's story about hanging with a kid from school, crashing on a couch so he doesn't have to tackle the roller-coaster road at night.

"Sure you don't want something to eat before you go?" He's pulling out a Comfort Meatloaf with Mashed Potatoes from the freezer, making a slit in the plastic.

"Think we're just gonna get some pizza," Fen tells him.

"There's pizza around here?" His dad looks hopeful, but also like he hasn't slept in a week. What's with the dark circles? Fen hadn't noticed them before, though the truth is, he hasn't been paying that much attention to his dad lately.

"*Frozen* pizza," Fen bluffs—no idea if there's actually a pizza place anywhere in the vicinity, though he doubts it. Miri's dad probably makes pizza from scratch. "Well, I'm pretty sure it's just frozen pizza." He grabs the backpack he'd already packed, but pauses before heading out the kitchen door. "Everything okay, Dad?" he asks. He understands how tough his dad's job can be, but dark circles usually mean an extra-tough case.

"Fine, fine." He's back to staring at the microwave, like that will make the four minutes go faster.

"Great. Just checking."

"Hold on a minute." His dad catches him just before he's shot out the door. "This guy you're hanging out with. Ever heard him mention the Wizard?"

"Wizard?" Fen smirks. "Harry Potter or Lord of the Rings?"

His dad grunts. "Never mind. Have fun tonight. But no funny business." He's grabbed a fork from the drawer and is emphasizing each word of that ridiculous phrase. "No. Funny. Business."

A mock salute. "Yes, sir."

Settling in behind the wheel, Fen takes a few deep breaths to calm his nerves. He can't believe what he's about to do, can't believe he's going to have a whole night with Miri. No interruptions. No dads. No Clay. Hopefully. Fen has a sudden vision of Clay standing at the end of Miri's driveway decked out in his head-to-toe camo, high-powered rifle at the ready, but he pushes that out of his head.

Fen takes the first curve out of his driveway too fast—*shit!*—and the tires make a squealing sound before he manages to pump the brakes.

"Cool it, dude. Now is not the time to die."

Slowing it down, taking it easy through the next curve and the next curve after that and then the perfect corkscrew. The truck keeps nosing toward the rusted guardrails, but Fen manages to keep the wheels mostly inside the white lines. His eyes flick to the gas gauge during a straight part, even though he knows it's almost full. He hardly ever drives the truck, really, except back and forth from his house to the shit hole. Usually it's the bike—Miri bringing him up here. Which makes him realize that he's never actually watched for the driveway on his own. What if he misses the turnoff? It's already getting dark, and he doesn't remember if there's a mailbox or some kind of marker.

Just when he thinks he's gone too far and he'll have to backtrack, he catches sight of a familiar flowery bush in the headlights— a honeysuckle, isn't that what Miri told him? He clicks on his left blinker, even though no one ever seems to be coming or going this far up.

CLAY

He hasn't slept for twenty-four hours at least, maybe more. But he doesn't feel tired. Not at all. More like he's finally awake, really awake, after all this time.

Clay remembers Cora never seeming to sleep and getting crazier and crazier, but he won't be like that. He's not going to keep snorting the stuff, just a little now and then. And he's definitely not going to start shooting it.

He'll snort a bit and then he'll stay up for one more night, one more backwoods party—*Clay! Clay! Clay!* That's what the shadows were chanting at the end—and then he'll crash. He'll rest hard before Poe gets back.

"Sunday," Poe had said. When they'd talked on the handheld—Clay trying to sound like his normal self. "We'll be back Sunday."

Poe had been pissed; Clay had had to keep apologizing about not checking in more. But that was okay. Because the news was good.

Poe staying gone till Sunday means Clay has more time. He'll just pop out for a few more bags of Wizard batch like he promised the shadows, and then he'll have plenty of time to figure out how to hide what's missing before Poe comes back.

"Where you going?"

He'd almost forgotten that Trent and Stevie are still with him, crashed on his stained and tufted-out couch, eyes zombied onto the TV screen. Not that there's anything to watch. Clay tried to tell them, but they ignored him, turned it on anyway, spent a long time adjusting the ancient bunny ears sticking up from the back until finally there were shimmering blobs of possibly human movement across the screen.

"You don't got Dish, dude?" Trent had asked straight off coming into the trailer, and Clay is glad it had gone back to "dude." He was getting tired of "retard" and might've had to punch Trent if he'd kept it up.

"No Xbox neither?" from Stevie.

"What do you do up here for fun?" Trent said.

"I read books," Clay'd told them, and that had made the donkey bray start up right away, and Trent was laughing too, and he sounded just like a snuffling pig.

"Where you going?" Trent is repeating the question and he's rising up from the couch like he's going to follow, but Clay shoves him—not hard, more like a warning.

"You can't come with me," Clay says. "I'll be back."

"Okay, that's cool!" Stevie hasn't moved from his corner of the couch, and he's got his hands up in the air. "That's cool with us, right, Trent?"

Trent doesn't answer, but he nods and sits back down.

Satisfied, Clay heads out the door, and the night swallows him whole like it always does, but somehow it's even *more*. Like he's melted into the darkness and he's part of it. Right away his eyes adjust and he is moving down those paths only he knows, only he could ever be able to navigate. Silent as the cougars that used to prowl these woods when Cora was a kid, cougars that got shot for trophies or scared off, every one, dying out from this part of the world.

"Maybe they'll come back," Miri had said when he'd told her about them years before. "Maybe one day they'll be here again."

And he'd agreed with her just to be nice, but maybe she's right and he'll see a cougar this very night—is that so impossible?—and they'll stare at each other inside the darkness, both of them with eyes glowing. And something will pass between them, a knowing that only creatures of the night can share, and then they'll move on, going their separate ways.

Something is glowing, far off, between the trees. There and then gone again. Clay goes perfectly still to listen to the far-off hum of the motor. A truck on Poe's driveway. A truck he knows, though he's never heard it all the way up here.

"Bambi grew a pair," Clay says out loud, and laughs at his own joke, until he realizes it's not funny. Bambi driving up here this late probably means he's going to stay. All night. Since Poe's not here.

Keep an eye on things, son.

Poe's instructions to him before he left.

"Can't do it." Clay turns, ducks onto the deer path that will take him to the lab. "Sorry, Poe."

MIRI

A feast—that's what she's set out for Fen. Basically because she couldn't choose from all the options Poe had left in the freezer. She wasn't sure what Fen would like. So she just went with a bit of everything.

"Whoa!" Fen says when he lays eyes on the spread. "That's a whole lotta food!"

"Yeah . . ." Embarrassed now. "Maybe it's overkill."

"No, it looks great! Your dad made all this himself? Like from scratch?"

"Poe likes to cook." Miri says the words and nearly laughs out loud. What if she blurted it all out right this very minute: *Poe isn't just good at cooking gourmet meals! He's good at cooking meth, too! Or at least that's what I hear! Haven't tried any myself.*

"It all smells really great," Fen says. "And I'm starving."

"Good! 'Cause there's plenty!"

They sit down at the places Miri already set—the nice plates and silverware, the cloth napkins. Even the candlesticks Cyrus carved from a downed cherry tree and the beeswax candles Junie makes herself.

Fancy-schmancy! She can almost hear Angel saying it. *Is this a date or something?*

Miri's never been on a date. She wonders if Fen has. Probably. It's not like he's been living under a rock his whole life like she has.

"Where should we start?" Fen asks, and Miri scoots the bowl of gnocchi forward.

"That's my favorite," she tells him, deciding to skip the whole "*yescchi*" thing, at least for now. "But if you don't like pasta, there's some steak tips with a mushroom sauce and some eggplant Parmesan and some chicken curry and a few slices of roast beef. Oh, and some chicken cacciatore."

"Hey, what's with the Band-Aid?" Fen gently catches her hand as she's waving at the different foods.

"Wounded in action. Maybe it's revenge of the spinach!" Letting him kiss her bandaged fingertip, pronouncing the "boo-boo all better now."

Fen tries everything—though only a tiny bit of the eggplant. "Not my favorite vegetable," he admits. "It's the texture, I guess. Just can't get past the mushiness."

When they're both stuffed, can't eat another bite, Fen helps clear the table, do the dishes. Miri feeds the leftover scraps to the hellhounds, along with their regular dry kibble. Fen hangs back as she moves from dog to dog. She can tell he's still wary, and she can't blame him.

"It's strange being here after dark," Fen admits as they head up the stairs, make their way back inside.

"Bad strange?" Miri asks, a ripple of worry surfacing.

"No! Sorry! Wrong word!" Slipping his fingers through hers. "Not strange at all, just . . . Usually we're saying goodbye when it gets dark. But now . . ."

"We don't have to say goodbye."

"We have all night."

Miri leads him down the hall to her room. Funny she's kept this space for last. It had felt so important to show Fen the garage where she spends most of her time, the framing table, her latest "creation." But this is important too, and Fen seems to understand. He goes still, his whole body, the way she's noticed he does when he's listening to a sound he hasn't heard before.

"This is my Panhead collection," she says, pausing in front of her collage of old black-and-white photos tacked to the wall. "What I'm modeling *my* Pan on." Waiting while he carefully studies each one, then moving on. "And this is what I might build next—a sand dragger." More photos, some in color, pages torn from various magazines. The starting line of a race; a few blurs of bikes in action, bikes sailing through the air, a couple of crashes. Her favorite— a group of guys (all guys, no gals, though she's read about a few female racers) posing together after a race, arms thrown around one another, completely covered in sand and mud, completely blasted with grit, except for the perfect pale circles around their eyes where their goggles had been.

"Sand draggers are made for racing," Miri explains. "They have a light frame but big, knobby wheels like dirt bikes." One photo is a silhouette—a rider perfectly balanced inside a desert moon. "That's what I want to do someday—desert racing. That's where I want to go—out west."

"I want to go with you."

Miri startles, she can't help it. Clay's words in Fen's mouth. A stab of joy; a stab of guilt, too.

"I mean, if you want me to." Fen nudges her shoulder. "Someday."

"Yeah, I want you to." Saying it quietly, turning to him. "How 'bout we leave right now?"

CLAY

"There's no food in here."

"What do you live on?"

Trent and Stevie have ransacked the kitchen while he was gone, cabinets and drawers open. Empty cracker boxes on the counter, each one spilling its hollow wrappers like filmy innards.

"This," Clay says, fishing the packets—ten in all—gently from his pockets, laying them in a line on the table.

"Holy shit, dude," Trent says.

Stevie is gaping. "Hey, man, you weren't lying."

"You think I'm a liar?" Clay's not sure where it came from, but the fire is inside him and he's got his hands around Stevie's neck before the guy even knows Clay's made it across the room. He slams Stevie's head into the wall and holds him there. Two feet off the ground at least, legs dangling, shoes kicking.

"Hey, it's okay. It's okay. Clay, buddy, it's okay." Trent is behind him, trying to talk him down. "Stevie's a moron. He says whatever comes into his head. We believe you, man. You're not a liar, no way."

The fire puffs out. Clay stares at the red face for a minute, the bugged-out eyes, Stevie's mouth, wide and gasping for air like a catfish flopped on the bank.

"Sorry," he says, releasing his grip, letting Stevie slide down the wall, fall over to the couch. "Sorry," he says again. "I'm not a liar."

"We know you're not, dude," Trent says. "You're cool." He nods back toward the table, all the pretty little packets. "And right now, you are a god to us."

Clay goes to the table, sits at the metal folding chair he found in the dump. He taps one packet closer, slides the rest farther away, into a pile. Then he yanks out his wallet, slips the license between his fingers, and starts crushing some of the bigger chunks, crushing and cutting. Not dividing, not yet.

"See, Stevie, see, he's a god, right? He's our buddy. And buddies help buddies, right? We're going to help big-time, dude, go into business together. Sell the crap out of this shit. And you'll put in a good word for us with the Wizard, right?"

Clay doesn't answer. But he does start cutting the crystal into three lines. Maybe not totally even. A little less for Stevie. Till he learns his manners.

"No food till you learn your manners," Cora would say when she was playing the bad mom. Keeping dinner from him. Not that she cooked dinner that much. It was always touch and go. He was always hungry.

Clay feels hungry now, but it's a distant hunger. He thinks of all the things he likes to eat at Poe's house, fancy things, like beef bourguignon and chicken cordon bleu and saltimbocca—names he never would've known except for Poe.

"Eat as much as you want, son." Clay thinks back to Poe saying that the very first meal, years ago when Poe found Clay running around in the woods, a kid with dirty clothes and dirty hair, a belly that had always, as long as Clay could remember, been painfully empty. "There's plenty here, son. Help yourself."

And that's just what Clay is doing now. Helping himself. Another bump of Wizard batch. Poe has been so generous throughout Clay's life. Would he really mind?

FEN

She was kidding, of course. About leaving *right now*.

"When I turn eighteen," she clarifies. "After I graduate. *If* I ever graduate from the shit hole."

"I'm still hoping we might talk Poe into starting up his Survival Home School again," Fen jokes, and Miri grunts.

"Don't hold your breath."

They move on to Miri's collection of geodes, rocks Fen had never really known about before. They seem to be everywhere in the knobs, lying by the side of the road or deer path. Plain brown on the outside, but when you smash one against another rock—surprise! A treasure inside—diamonds. Well, not real diamonds. Just quartz crystals—clear but sometimes with a purplish hue. Amethyst, she's told him.

"They have coyotes out west just like here," Fen says, tuning in to the faint yipping that's started outside Miri's window, somewhere farther up the knob.

"You've already been out west?" Her voice is a little sad.

"Just for a year or so. Montana. I think I told you. Honestly don't remember much." He takes her hand. "It'll be different when we go there together."

"What about college?" Eyes narrowing. "I bet you have plans."

"Not really. Haven't told my parents yet, but I want to find a place with some kind of digital sound program." He shrugs. "I'd like to learn more about technical stuff, how to make my sound-scapes better." He watches her. "Maybe there're schools like that out west."

Miri's eyes go bright. "And I could get a job working at a garage."

"*You* don't want to go to college?"

"Probably not." Glancing away, seeming embarrassed.

"You can decide later." Putting his arms around her. "You can do whatever the hell you want. Long as we're together."

Miri is shorter than he is, smaller, but their bodies seem to fit perfectly together. Crazy to think how awkward it felt that first time, getting onto Miri's bike. How awkward it felt to wrap his arms around this girl he'd just met, a girl who'd seemed to appear out of nowhere. He remembers how loosely he tried to hold her at first, out of politeness.

"Hold on tight!" Miri kept telling him as they climbed higher and higher. "Hold on tight!"

It's what he did then, and pretty much every day after.

Hold on tight!

It's what he does now because he can't ever imagine letting Miri go.

CLAY

Music blaring through the trees like before. That's how you find the parties. No exact location given, just a vague notion of which knob, which patch of woods, which fork in the river. And then you listen; you follow the sound.

Lynyrd Skynyrd still rules supreme. Even though it's grandpa music. Great-grandpa music more like. All those old rockers, dead and gone. Half of them smashed to bits in a plane crash—isn't that right? Or most of them. A flash of Cora's face, the tears streaming down her cheeks as she told him. A tragedy, she called it, and she was crying though the story was old even by then, dusty as decomposed shit, so why did it matter anymore anyway? But of course Cora was high, and that meant that anything could set her off—crying or laughing or screaming, you never knew which way it would go.

"They were rock stars." He remembers her sobbing out the words. "The world at their feet. And then they were gone."

She'd start singing along, of course. All that stuff about the bird flying, needing to be free.

Irony, she told him. Cora wasn't dumb either, but she liked to pretend she was. Quit school, got pregnant. The song is ironic because the singer is talking about being free, and then he's dead.

"All right! Here's the big guy, the king!" somebody is shouting from way up on the ledge that juts out over the creek. "Let's get this party started."

And then it's a slow stampede, and Trent and Stevie handle the swish of bills while Clay lets the small squares of magic flow from his fingers. He is a god, just like Stevie said before. And he loves his people right now, right this minute. The ones slapping him on the shoulder after the exchange, the girls leaning in to flutter their lips against his cheek, his neck. He is a god, and when his pockets are empty and his people are satisfied, he climbs up onto that ledge, high as he can go, and he doesn't have to tell the other guys to get down, they just do. And he sits and reaches for the plastic square in his pocket—the last one, but that's okay. He's a benevolent leader, a good provider, and he will provide more while he covers what he's taken from the Wizard. A plan is forming.

Clay taps out some of the crystal—not much, just a quick bump—along the webbing between his thumb and pointer and brings it to his nose. The plan is already downloading in his head—fast, like one of those computers from the future, fast, like he's a genius or something. Maybe he's always been a genius and those teachers in that stupid school just didn't know how to handle him. Maybe Poe didn't know how to handle him either.

MIRI

She slips the T-shirt up and over his shoulders, runs her hands down his smooth arms, shoulders, chest.

"No tattoos," she breathes.

"Disappointed?" he asks, and she firmly shakes her head.

"Not at all."

Then she's tugging at her own shirt, revealing all the empty spaces like a blank slate. She wants to *be* a blank slate. She wants to peel off the layers, drop each one at her feet. She wants to reveal herself to Fen, nothing to hide. At least not tonight.

CLAY

Some girl's on him. Pushing her body up against him, boobs pressing into his chest, mouth suckering on his neck, and it doesn't feel bad. He doesn't push her away, but sways with the music the way they've been doing for a few minutes or maybe a few hours, he has no idea. It's still dark, still night, so that's something. Carrie. Or Kenzie. He can't remember. Some girl he knew from school. Some girl who wouldn't give him the time of day back then. Wouldn't give him the time of day now if he hadn't been the king of the party tonight. But that's okay. Because it feels good. The way she's rubbing herself on him, the way her mouth is working up his neck and along his jaw, closer to his. Her lips are candied—some kind of flavored lip gloss, and it's not a bad taste, not a bad feeling, being swallowed up, that's how it feels. Swallowed up and part of somebody else for a change, and he wishes it was Miri but it's not, and that's okay for now.

FEN

Heart pounding, blood rushing, neurons zapping. Or is it synapses zapping? He can't remember. Sixth-grade science, maybe? Learning about how the body works, how it functions. All those systems. Respiratory, digestive, skeletal, muscular, cardiovascular.

Synapses—that's the structure, right? Inside the nervous system. And the neurons are the transmitters. All those little chemical and electrical charges being transmitted inside the human body, inside *his* body. Zapping. Sparking—exactly like the tiny fireworks he witnessed when Miri was welding.

What if he could capture all that? Some special mic hooked directly into his body, recording how haywire everything gets just from one simple touch, Miri's touch.

Overdrive—a word he's heard Miri use. Something to do with engines, revving a motor, pushing a machine to its limit. Overdrive— a sound term as well. Musicians amp up the bass on purpose sometimes to make a particular riff fuzzy, distorted.

The Sound of Love.

What he would call this crazy internal soundscape that's happening inside his own body. If he could capture it, record it, play it back. Give it to Miri as a gift, some kind of proof: this is happening; this is real.

The Sound of Love.

CLAY

Who cooks for you? Who cooks for you all?

There it is again. The call. Maybe it really is his and Miri's owl, all grown up. Maybe it's a sign she'll forget Bambi and realize how much Clay loves her, how much he can give her. Especially now that he could work with Poe, be a kind of equal.

Who cooks for you? Who cooks for you all?

Or maybe it's a different kind of sign. Like a death is coming. That's what Cora always said.

Your granny saw an owl out her kitchen window, and the next day Pop-pop was lying dead on the floor.

"Those old hoot owls give me the creeps, dude," Trent says now. They're coming back from the party, walking through the woods.

"I know, right?" Stevie answers. "Like they're crying or something. Ghosts crying in the night."

Clay moves ahead on the trail, wishes he could lose them, forget about them. He can still taste that cherry lip gloss. He wipes his sleeve across his mouth, wanting to get rid of that, too. The owl has made him want to go to Miri. Right now. Tell her how he feels. Explain it with this new clarity, this new joy. He doesn't have to be ashamed anymore. Like he's not her equal, not Poe's equal. He's been a god, these last couple of days, and he can keep being a god if he wants to, if he makes it happen.

"Hey, wait up," Stevie calls. "You're moving too fast. It's fucking dark out here and I don't know where I'm going."

"Yeah, hold up," Trent calls. "We're not all knob-billies here, am I right, Stevie? Some of us are used to walking on flat land like regular folk."

Now Clay does want to stop. He wants to wait for Trent to catch up and then swing around and punch him, hard as he can. He wants to fucking drop Trent where he stands and leave him in the dark. And Stevie would stay because he'd be scared shitless and they'd both just cower together in the woods being scared of old hoot owls till it got light enough for them to find their way back down the knob, back to their *flat* land.

"Maybe he shorted us, that's what I'm thinking." Trent is still talking. "'Cause I'm running on empty, but retard over there seems to be flying. Makes you wonder, right?"

"Yeah, what's the deal, Clay?" Stevie chimes in from farther back. "Thought you were gonna be solid on hooking us up from now on. Thought you were in tight with the Wizard."

"I don't need the Wizard."

Clay is not even sure he said it out loud—or loud enough for the idiots following him to hear. But he must've because Stevie is laughing that donkey-bray laugh, and of course Trent is joining in, snuffling like some old pig. And together they are so loud, just so goddamn loud when the woods are meant for silence, or not silence exactly, but quiet reverence—yeah, that's the word, right? It's amazing how his brain can produce words he didn't even know were there. Quiet reverence for all the life hidden inside the dark, all the wild things just trying to be wild without two jackasses braying and snorting and ruining the world for everybody.

"I said I don't need the Wizard." Clay stops and turns.

"Whoa!" Trent nearly crashes into him and then jolts again when Stevie bumps and stalls. "What the hell? What you saying, re— I mean *dude?*"

Dude. Retard. Does it really matter? They're both said in the same tone; Clay sees it now, hears it. A mocking tone. Like they've just been humoring him all along.

You're a god to us.

Trent's words from before. And it hits Clay how it's not true. Once a retard, always a retard, right? Exactly the way these two would think.

"Come on," Clay says, turning but not rushing ahead like before, giving these two assholes—these two losers who can't even walk down a clear path in the dark—a chance to follow. "I'll show you."

FEN

The sound isn't nearly as loud as he thought it would be. He only catches it because he's already awake, watching Miri as she sleeps. He carefully feels for his phone on the bedside table. Doesn't want to shift, wake her.

Big Red crows a second time, and then a third. It's a ragged sound—not the brave *cock-a-doodle-doo* of cartoons and movies. Almost sad, mournful. The birds just outside the window are bolder—trills and chirps, loud and insistent, brashly rippling up and down the scale.

"The dawn chorus."

Miri is awake; she's blinking slowly at him—a sleepy cat. Tawny tangled hair spread out across the pillow. A lion. He leans in and softly kisses her, not caring about his fuzzy mouth, praying Miri doesn't care either.

"That's what you call it," she murmurs. "The dawn chorus."

"The dawn chorus really upstaged Big Red. I barely heard him."

"He's getting old," Miri admits. "Not as loud as he used to be." She watches him for a moment—sleepy eyes. "Are you disappointed? Big Red's the whole reason you stayed overnight."

"Not the whole reason." He leans in again, but this time she turns her head away.

"Poe will be back soon," she says in a voice that's hardly there.

"Tomorrow, right?"

She nods.

"So, we've got the whole day."

Miri still has her head turned, gazing toward the window, a pale square of light in the dim room, barely morning yet. The crack of dawn. "We have today," she says, turning, giving him a thin smile—no gap—then putting her mouth to his.

MIRI

She leaves him once he's fallen asleep again, but not before she's grabbed his phone. She goes down the hall, closes the bathroom door, locks it behind her.

At this point, she's watched Fen enough to know how it works, which app to open, which button to press. She talks quietly but distinctly. She says what she needs to say.

When she's done, she slips the phone back where it was. She stands at the edge of the bed, staring down at Fen for a long time. She knows she could stand there forever. But she makes herself turn, makes herself go down the hall again, start the new day.

FEN

Something's shifted. Miri's still *here*—she's talking, she's laughing, she's taking his hand when he reaches for her, she's kissing him (a *lot* of kissing)—and yet she's *gone*.

Is it something he said? Something he did? Something he didn't do? He can't figure it out. Maybe it's just that she needs some space, a little time alone. They've never actually spent this many uninterrupted hours together.

"Hey, I'm going to go down and check in with my dad," he says late in the afternoon. "But I'll come back quick as I can."

"That's okay." They're in the garage now, and Miri's examining some cables on the MIG, said she noticed they were loose yesterday. "I've got a lot of garden stuff to do before Poe gets back."

"Yeah, I can help with that," he offers.

"It'll probably go faster if I'm alone," Miri says, not looking at him. "I can get more done if I'm focused." Unhooking a cable, plugging it in again. "And I have a lot of welding to do after that. I'm behind on the Pan. Really got to make some progress on it."

"Hey, you trying to get rid of me?" He says it as a joke, but she doesn't laugh, doesn't respond at all. "What's up, Miri?" he asks finally. "What's wrong?"

"Nothing's *wrong.*" Voice slightly raised, a flash of annoyance. "I have a lot to do. Can't just mess around all day."

Okayyyyy. Wow!

Is that all they've been doing here? Just "messing around"? *What the hell?*

Fen glances away from Miri, trying to work it out. Did they go too far last night, this morning? Not far enough? Fen hadn't wanted to rush things more than they'd already been rushed. Hadn't wanted to do anything Miri—or Fen himself—wasn't ready for. Looks like that was the right decision. Now that she's gone all alien clone.

"Okay, guess I'll go grab my stuff," he says, turning, giving her a chance to stop him and when she doesn't, heading up the stairs, into the house. He grabs his backpack with the laptop—he didn't bring much.

One or two of the hellhounds shift as he comes back down the steps, rattling their chains, but otherwise pay him no mind. Like he's not even there.

"I'm leaving," he calls to Miri. "But I've still got the walkie-talkie," he can't help but add. "So I'll check in with you."

"Yeah, fine," Miri says. She's pulling on the welding apron, reaching for the helmet.

"Okay, see you . . . later."

This time she does turn, glance at him. And the hair on the back of his neck actually rises. Because it's Miri standing there looking at him. But at the same time, it's *not* Miri. It's like that really old *Body Snatchers* movie he watched with his mom once. Aliens creating perfect replicas of humans, clones actually grown in gardens. (Did he see any suspiciously large pods growing between the rows this morning?) Aliens taking over the Earth, the only way to tell the difference: their cold, emotionless behavior.

"Miri . . . ," he begins, but she's already turning away, pulling on the welder's helmet, flipping the switch on the MIG, the ear-splitting sound becoming a force field around her.

MIRI

With the helmet on, there's no chance of Fen seeing her face, seeing the tears welling up in her eyes, falling down her cheeks. With the MIG going, there's no chance of him hearing her softly saying the words, "I'm sorry. I'm sorry for being such an asshole, such a coward."

It takes forever, but finally he does walk out of the garage, does leave her alone like she asked him to, alone with her beloved creations—beauties or monsters, she's not even sure. Maybe she should ditch the Pan for now, start on the sand dragger. Maybe she could head out west sooner than she thought. Does she really have to be eighteen? Would Poe come after her, or let her go?

Miri remembers how she first learned about desert racing. She was flipping through some old magazines that had piled up in a corner of the garage over the years. There was an article with those photos she'd ripped out and tacked to her wall, lots of quotes— riders talking about how a big part of the thrill of desert racing was that the races were at night, in the dark. How dangerous it all was, *life and death* dangerous. According to one guy, you'd be going flat and fast (one record was two hundred miles per hour), but there'd always be this chance you'd crash down a fifty-foot-deep mine shaft nobody'd marked on a map, or you'd smash into a giant boulder. "Lots of guys were lost," one racer said. "Lots of guys just never made it to the finish line."

Miri *does* want to make it to the finish line; she wants to get out of Paradise, she wants some kind of future beyond the knobs. And she wants that future with Fen because . . . well, because she loves him.

Miri *loves* Fen.

Yeah, it's crazy; yeah, it's "way too soon," as some people would say. But it's real, not just some crush, not some phase. Miri feels it deep in her heart, deep in her very bones. She loves Fen, and that's why she has to let him go.

There's a reason you build your sand dragger's frame light and small—so you can go faster, farther. You'd never race with a passenger wrapped around you—the thought is completely absurd, laughable. You'd never weight yourself down if the whole purpose was to fly.

FEN

When he gets home, his dad's not even there.

*Had to run. Work. Back extra late. Plenty of dinners in
the freezer. No funny business while I'm gone!*

"Funny business" underlined three times, of course.

Fen thinks about turning around, climbing back into the truck,
heading straight up the knob to Miri. He thinks about calling her
on the walkie-talkie.

Can't just mess around all day.

"Shit." Fen goes to his room, flops on the bed. "Shit."

Inside his head, he replays everything from when he first
arrived at Paradise last night and they ate all that food—did he
make a pig of himself? Probably, but that hadn't seemed to bother
her. They'd done some basic chores like feeding the hellhounds,
closing the chickens into their coop for the night. Then they'd

spent the rest of the time in her room—they'd basically never left.

Fen pulls out his phone, thumbs to the Big Red recording, listens to the muffled crow. *"The dawn chorus,"* he hears Miri say. *"That's what you call it . . . the dawn chorus."*

He closes his eyes, listening to the dialogue, like he and Miri are in a movie.

"We have today."

Miri's last words. And then the muffled sound of their kissing. A Sound of Love soundscape. Not the one he'd envisioned, a recording of his neurons and synapses—as if that were even possible—but a sad substitute. It feels wrong to be listening to their morning make-out session, like he's some kind of perv. He's about to erase this particular section, the end of the clip, but he can't. What if this was the last time he kisses Miri? What if this is the only proof he has—what he thought was love?

"Shit." He rolls over to grab his laptop—might as well download everything so he can archive it. He starts with chickens keening and some bees buzzing. There's a couple of different takes on that bird that keeps repeating "Bob-*white*" so clear, and then there's the cicadas droning on and on. He closes his eyes to focus but he must doze off, because nearly an hour has passed when he checks his phone again, and that's when he notices a short clip after the dawn chorus, the kissing. Not long, less than a minute. Probably just a butt recording, like a butt dial, easy to do sometimes. Nothing important. But then he goes completely still.

"Hey, Fen."

Miri's voice, low, whispering.

"Sorry to tell you this way . . . but I just can't . . . it's hard enough . . . looking you in the eye. But you deserve to know the truth about me . . . about Poe."

Fen jerks to sitting, looks at the phone in his hands, hits the stop button. He takes a couple of deep breaths. Then he adjusts the earbuds so he won't miss a word, replays Miri's voice. Listens to the whole thing again. And again. And then one more time.

"Shit." He jumps up and paces the room. "Shit, shit, shit."

Then he goes down the hall, stands in front of his dad's door.

"Shit."

His hand is on the knob; he hesitates. But only for a moment.

Fen knows his dad keeps work files at home, has always known. But he's honestly never been tempted to look at them before today, before now.

A stack of manila folders—the one marked *The Wizard* isn't even on top. In fact, it's basically at the bottom of the pile. But it's thicker than the rest, chock-full of photos.

Miri's house, the garage, the chicken coop—everything taken from above. He recognizes the layout, the camouflage netting. He sees the hellhounds chained up at intervals in the yard. There are more aerial photos, Sharpie arrows pointing to certain spots that are circled. The marked places enlarged—extra-blurry treetops.

Next up are a couple of photos taken from a distance—Clay pumping gas at the BP station. Then a few shots of a super-skinny blond woman in short-shorts and a skimpy tank top crossing various parking lots.

Finally, it's the Wizard himself. Poe. Has to be. Something about the shape of his face, his mouth, reminds Fen of Miri. But his eyes are different. Something weird about them. And he has brown hair, not Miri's reddish gold. Brown with streaks of gray, brown and gray stubbling his cheeks and chin. Poe is probably the same age as Fen's dad, by the looks of it, but his body is harder, he's much more fit. When Poe's not wearing a black leather jacket, his tats are visible. Full-on sleeves, bright ink swirling down his arms, stopping at his wrists.

Miri's in the next few shots. Most of the photos are blurred because she's on her bike or getting off her bike or striding across the shit hole parking lot with the vaping buzzards in the background.

Fen stands there for a long time, flipping through the photos, trying to make out some notes scrawled on the back—his dad's handwriting is illegible.

"Shit."

Fen sets the file back at the bottom, straightens the pile, and heads out the door. He tries to reach his dad on his cell phone once he's inside the truck, bumping down the gravel driveway, but like always, the call doesn't go through.

Shit.

He pulls onto the main road, lets the tires squeal around the first turn. It's not like he has any kind of plan—what he's going to do back at Paradise. All he knows is that he's got to get to Miri before Poe—or his DEA agent dad—does.

MIRI

She'd had a feeling in her gut—that's why she was such an asshole to Fen. Or part of the reason.

"Surprise!" Poe is shouting out the window after he's brought his truck to a skidding-in-the-gravel halt. "I see you in there!" Peering into the garage. "Come on out! Got you a present!"

Miri does as she's told, wiping her hands on a towel. Her brain flits to the house—nothing left of Fen's, right? She's pretty sure he took his backpack with him when he left.

"Lookee here!" Poe is crowing, holding up a vintage rear fender with a hinged tail, plus a vintage headlamp. "I saw them and I couldn't resist. Thought they'd be perfect for the Pan!" He's striding into the garage to set his gift down next to the framing table, then he's circling it, nodding his approval. "Looking good!" he says. "Lots of progress!"

Angel has followed Poe into the garage. She grabs Miri from behind—tiny but weirdly strong—lifts her straight into the air.

"We missed you!" Angel cries, breath smelling of beer. "Your dad couldn't wait to get home and tell you his news."

"What news?" Miri watches Poe as he continues to circle the Pan. He looks different somehow, but she can't put a finger on it. Same clothes, same haircut. Same scruff with gray peppering the brown.

"Wanted to tell Clay, too. Where is he?" Making a big show of looking around, like he's in a game of hide-and-seek. "If you're working on a bike, he's usually right here beside you."

"He's . . ." Before she can think of what to say, what excuse to make as to why Clay isn't here, why he hasn't been here much at all, the sound of gravel crunching under wheels makes them all turn toward the door.

"Expecting somebody?" Poe's eyes laser in on Miri, but when she doesn't answer right away, he turns, arm reaching back, finding what's always hidden there: the Governor.

FEN

It's just like his first trip to Paradise. Gun pointed at his chest, dude telling him to put his hands in the air.

This time it's scarier, though. Because he knows. The dude is Poe, aka the Wizard. Fen understands everything now.

"Search him!" Poe's voice cuts through the air, and Fen doesn't know what to expect, but then the woman comes forward—the skinny blonde from the photos. She's short—tiny, in fact—but Fen doesn't doubt her strength as she brusquely runs her hands up and down, front and back.

"Clean," she calls, turning sharply away, but not before giving Fen a quick wink.

Weird.

"Of course he's clean!" Miri has placed herself between Fen and the gun. Would she take a bullet for him? Would Poe actually *put a bullet* in Fen? "He's just a kid from school. A new kid. You don't know him."

"Yeah, well, what's this *new kid* doing all the way up here?" Poe isn't lowering the gun. "Is he a friend of yours?"

The question hangs in the air, and for a crazy moment Fen wonders if Miri's going to deny it. But then she nods.

"Yeah. He's a friend." She turns to Fen, and her eyes are flashing like they do so often, but this time it's different. They're flashing with fear. "He just came up here . . . to borrow something . . . for school."

"Is that right?" Poe is staring right at him, and his eyes aren't the same color—that's what it is. Something Fen has never seen before. "What's your name, son?"

"Fen," Miri answers for him. "His name's Fen."

"Fen," Poe repeats, more to himself.

"It's a family name," Fen offers lamely. What does Poe care?

But Poe *does* seem to change, soften the tiniest bit.

"A family name, huh?" He lowers the gun—*thank God!* "Okay." Shrugging like it was all a simple misunderstanding. "You hungry?" Poe asks, like a normal dad, like he didn't just have Fen frisked. "I'm starving," he says without waiting for an answer. "Thought I'd whip something up real fast. So you can stay for dinner . . . *Fen.*" Giving extra weight to the name.

"He just came up to borrow something . . . a book . . . for school," Miri is saying, exasperation in her voice. "I'm sure he needs to get home."

Poe is tucking the gun behind him, under his shirt, into his waistband, same way Fen's own dad carries his Beretta.

"And I'm sure your *friend* can stay for dinner," Poe tells her. "In fact, I insist."

CLAY

I'm burping the baby.

What Cora used to say. Holding that two-liter plastic Coke bottle as careful as she would a baby—did she hold Clay that careful when he was just born? Jiggling the bottle a little—not too much!—and then releasing the top just the tiniest bit.

I'm burping the baby.

And now Clay is doing the same thing. A Mountain Dew two-liter he hadn't gotten rid of yet—taken along with all of Poe's recycling. A greenish baby, like an alien, balanced gently between his palms. Cora's grandbaby—a joke he could say out loud, share with Trent and Stevie, but won't because they wouldn't get it. They'd probably give a donkey bray and a pig snort just for show and then laugh for real about it later.

What was that retard talking about? Grandbabies?

Got me, dude.

"How long's this gonna take?"

A real voice, the real Trent talking. Whispering, because Clay told them before he started that any little vibration could set things off. He didn't mean talking, of course. It's not like talking is going to cause the bottle to explode, which would not be good because of the propane tank that heats the stove, the water, the furnace in the winter. But forget about that—Cora never gave a damn. The trick is, you just have to be careful to shake the bottle enough but not too much, to keep burping it—unscrewing the cap—when the pressure inside the bottle builds up. No big deal. Clay would prefer silence, though, so he gives Trent a look that means *shut the fuck up*, and amazingly, Trent does.

"Sure you know what you're doing?" Stevie had asked when they first got back to the trailer and Clay explained what would happen. "Why do you have to cook it yourself? Why can't we just go up to the Wizard's and get more? If you're such a big deal. Why you got to shake and bake?"

"Poe's gone for a few days," Clay had explained. "Can't take more without asking."

"But you'll hook us up when he gets back?" Stevie said, and Clay nodded.

"And you sure you know what you're doing?" Trent demanded.

"Born knowing," Clay answered, a joke mostly. But not totally.

Who knows what gets passed down, mama to babe, through the womb? All that time spent inside Cora when she was undoubtedly cooking, baby or no. All that time watching her through his little baby eyes. Open but not really focused. Isn't that the way it is with babies? Human and animal alike? Nothing clear at first and then the sight gets better, stronger, over time? And then once the focus comes, watching but not understanding, just mimicking the motions maybe, mimicking what the parent does.

Clay has definitely done this before. Jiggling a bottle just so, twisting the cap just enough. Maybe it didn't have liquid in it—sloshing and fizzing and forming chunks the way it does now. Maybe he would just mirror what Cora was doing with her own two-liter. But all that watching and pretending—it was preparing him for this moment of one-batching it for real.

MIRI

"I was thinking saltimbocca."

First thing Poe says after they're all inside—naturally. Who else but Poe would hold a gun on somebody one minute, offer to cook him a special meal the next?

Miri catches Fen's eye, tries to silently convey so many things at once. How sorry she is for being a jerk earlier, how sorry she is for chasing him away. How sorry she is for not having the guts to tell Fen in person about Poe.

How sorry she is that Fen didn't stay away like she asked him to—as far away from her, from Paradise, as he possibly can.

"I'm just going to wash up some, get the road dirt off me." Angel sweeps through, carrying her overnight bag. "Back in a jiff." Turning to Miri, she mouths, "He's cute!" before disappearing around the corner.

Miri checks to make sure Poe didn't just catch that exchange, but he's opened the fridge door, rummaging around inside. "I'm so sorry," she whispers while Poe's view's blocked, while she has time. "I'm—"

"It's okay. I understand," Fen whispers back, cutting her off. "There's something I have to tell you."

"What is it?" Miri asks, but the fridge door slams shut and she scoots away.

"Saltimbocca!" Poe's voice booms out. "Do you know what the word means, Fen?" He's at the counter now, bustling, laying things out.

"No, sir, I don't."

"Miri?" Lifting his chin to her. "Would you care to enlighten your friend?"

Miri wants to explode. But she knows she needs to stay calm for Fen's sake, for his safety.

"'Jump into the mouth,'" she says flatly. "Saltimbocca means 'jump into the mouth.'"

"Exactly!" Triumphant, ignoring her obvious lack of enthusiasm. "'Jump into the mouth'! A dish so delicious, it will actually jump into your mouth for you."

"Sounds great, sir." Fen smiles. "Can't wait to taste it."

"Don't worry about the 'sir.'" Waving it off. "We're all friends here, right? Just call me Poe."

"Yes, s—" Fen catches himself. "I mean, Poe."

"Good!" Settling in at the counter. "Now, the thing I like about saltimbocca—besides how delicious it is, of course—is that it's so simple. Hardly takes any time." Poe reaches for a knife. "And yet, it's a good dish to serve because it seems like you've put a lot more effort into it than you have." Using the knife to point toward the stool directly across the island counter. "Take a seat, Fen. We'll have a little chat while I'm fixing the food."

"Sure." Fen eases down, flashing Miri an *I've got this* smile, but she can tell he's not totally sure. Poe is such an odd mix of charm and menace, it's confusing, even for Miri.

"The original recipe calls for veal," Poe is saying, "but Miri's never been a fan of that—the whole idea of eating baby cows never sat well with her. Though she's not a squeamish girl by nature. She's helped butcher a cow plenty of times."

"You've helped butcher a cow?" Fen's eyes are doing that puppy-dog thing again.

"Not really." She glares at Poe. "I was just there. I didn't do any actual butchering."

"We do all the butchering over at June and Cyrus's place," Poe explains to Fen. "Cows, pigs, goats. Different times of the year. We help each other, and then we share the meat, freeze it for the future."

Miri can tell Fen's pretty grossed out by the idea of a butchering party. She's thinking of how to change the subject when Poe asks Fen if he's met June and Cyrus.

"Our neighbors across the knob?"

Fen shakes his head. "No, but Miri's told me about them."

"You didn't go see them while I was away?" Poe's watching Miri now.

"I was busy with the garden," she answers, holding his gaze. It's not a lie, just not the total truth.

"I noticed that on the way in." Poe nods, approving. "You got a lot done. Good job." Pausing. "Did you have some help?" His voice is casual, but it's an act, Miri can tell. "Clay, for instance?"

She takes a moment to think of how to answer. "Clay hasn't been around much," she finally replies, more of the truth.

"Have to admit, I'm not too happy about that." Less casual now. "Clay's supposed to be doing a job, watching out for you."

"I don't need a babysitter." Miri can't hide her own irritation. "I'm not a kid anymore."

"So you keep telling me." Poe gives her a pointed look, then goes to the fridge, grabs a beer, offers one to Fen.

"No thanks," Fen responds.

"Good man." Poe takes a long pull at the bottle before starting in on the gourmet chef routine again. "So, here's what I do for saltimbocca, Fen. I cut the beef into thin strips. . . ." Demonstrating as he goes. "Same thing for the prosciutto and mozzarella." Pulling out the other ingredients from the fridge, and then snapping his fingers like he's just remembering. "Hey, Mir, run out and grab me some thyme and sage and rosemary from the garden."

Miri hesitates. She doesn't want to leave the kitchen.

"Please," he adds. "And some greens for a salad."

"Sure." Miri glances to Fen.

"Don't worry! I'll give this young man a job too." Poe gives a sly smile. He slides the block of mozzarella across the counter. "Here, son, cut up the mozzarella for me, would you? Thin slices like this."

"No problem."

"I'll just be a second," Miri says, more for Fen's benefit, then heads out the door.

She can't believe it's nearly dark already—when did that happen? She wonders if Clay will show up now that Poe is home, wonders what he'll say, how he'll act. She picks through the herbs, knowing she needs to rush back inside, but feeling the relief of having even a tiny moment to herself to think.

She needs to get Fen out of here; she needs to come up with a story.

A book, like she thought of before. She'll grab a book from her room, one she thinks they might possibly be reading in school. As soon as dinner's over, she'll say something about having a giant paper to do, how they both need time to work on it, insist Fen goes back home.

FEN

It's pretty frickin' surreal. Sitting right across from Poe aka the Wizard while he slices and dices, keeps a constant banter going like some celebrity chef. His favorite brand of knife (Zwilling), his favorite type of skillet (cast-iron).

"I knew a Fen once," Poe says, and those eyes! It's not just the fact that they're two different colors, it's their intensity. Their ferocity. Not all the time, but now. Right this moment. Like Poe goes mutant. Like he's got welding torches for eyes, and Fen's afraid he's gonna burn out his retinas if he keeps staring.

"Really? It's not that common a name."

"No, it's not." Poe focuses on what he's doing for a bit, then looks up again. "Have you met Clay?"

Fen hesitates. He feels the heat rising from his neck—what's the right answer here?

"What'd I miss?" Miri asks, bursting through the door with her hands full of green things.

"I was just asking Fen if he'd met Clay," Poe explains.

Miri shakes her head firmly. "No. He hasn't."

"Hmmmm." Poe takes the herbs from Miri, rinses and chops, then reaches for a brown glass bottle sitting on the shelf above the stove. "I mostly use olive oil when I'm cooking." Shooting a look to Fen to make sure he's following along. "Sadly, that's one thing I can't get local. Olives don't do well here. And I'm particular to the olive oil made in the Tuscany region of Italy. I get it sent by the case so I never run out."

"That must be pricey," Fen says, though how would he know? He's never bought olive oil, not sure if his mom buys olive oil. But he figures he just needs to keep the conversation going.

"Worth every penny. The olive oil they sell in, say, Kroger or Walmart, it would be a joke in Italy. Literally the bottom of the barrel, the dregs."

"Never knew that."

"You learn something new every day," Poe says. "Isn't that right?" Again, with the welding-torch eyes. Fen wonders if he'll be blind by the time he leaves here—*with* Miri, that's the plan.

"Yes, sir—" he says, clicking his tongue. "Yes, *Poe*, I guess it is."

Poe starts placing the beef he's already sliced into the skillet almost tenderly—oil hissing and crackling. "You want to brown it evenly, on each side," he tells Fen. "Just a couple of minutes. Not long. You never want to overcook something. Don't you agree?"

"Honestly, I don't know that much about cooking," Fen admits.

"Always a good skill to learn. How to feed yourself." Poe glances over his shoulder at Miri. "You're washing those greens?"

Miri holds them up in answer, water dripping.

"Great!" Poe says. "And some dressing as well?"

"On it."

The sound of sizzling takes over as Poe flips the meat a couple of times. It's strange watching Poe and Miri as they work side by side, almost in sync. At one point, Miri reaches for the olive oil, and her dad automatically hands it over. If Fen didn't know the whole story, he'd swear these two were close.

We used to be. What Miri said early on.

Fen wishes Miri had told him about Poe sooner. But he understands. How hard it must be for Miri; how hard it would be to admit your dad is a criminal, some kind of drug lord.

And how will Miri react when Fen tells her *his* news?

So, yeah, my dad can help you, but I guess that means he'll be putting your dad behind bars.

How twisted is that? How absurd? What are the chances? Fen and Miri meeting, hanging out, falling for each other, all without knowing that their dads are on opposite sides of a great big divide. Something out of a movie, or a play. Shakespeare comes to mind. *Romeo and Juliet*, feuding families and all that.

"And voilà!" Poe takes the pan off the stove, flourishing it in front of Fen. "As promised, a delicious meal, in no time flat."

"Smells great!" Fen says truthfully. His stomach is rumbling even though it's also half tied in knots at being here with the Wizard, at trying to figure out how to get Miri away.

"We'll set the table," Miri says, catching Fen's eye, giving a tiny nod toward the dining room. "Fen can help."

"Good idea," Poe agrees.

As soon as they're around the corner, Miri moves in close. "We'll finish eating, and then you'll tell Poe you need to leave," she whispers. "Tell him your dad is waiting for you at home. That he has a strict curfew or something."

"I want you to come with me," he insists, but she's shaking her head.

"I can't."

"My dad can help you, Miri. Get you away from here, protect you." Fen takes her hand. "My dad knows all about the Wizard—"

Miri jerks her hand away, gives him a piercing look. "Who *is* your dad?"

But before Fen can answer, Poe is coming around the corner, carrying the dish that will supposedly *jump into their mouths.*

MIRI

Her hands have started trembling. Miri tries to cut the meat on her plate but gives up, afraid Poe will notice. Who is Fen's dad? How long has Fen known the truth?

"Not hungry?" Poe *is* watching her, zeroing in. "Feeling okay, darlin'?"

"Fine." Miri takes a breath, steadies herself as best she can. "It's good," she says after she's managed to cut the tiniest bite, stick it into her mouth, chew.

"It's amazing, Poe!" Fen is extra enthusiastic, trying to grab the focus, she can tell. "Best thing I've ever tasted. Truly."

And Poe is charmed by that. "Glad you like it, son," he says, and Miri gives Fen a grateful glance. "And now that we're all sitting here enjoying our meal, I'd like you to tell us a little about yourself, Fen. New kid, huh? Not from around here—that's pretty obvious."

"I've been living with my mom in Detroit," Fen answers.

"Motor City!" Angel pumps a fist in the air.

"Motor City," Fen echoes.

"Big change for you, I'd say," Poe observes.

"Yeah, pretty big change," Fen agrees.

"Up here in the knobs, you're so removed from everything. So remote."

"Definitely remote," Fen says, and Angel is jumping in, talking about how she'd prefer to live in a city, how she hates not being able to go shopping more.

"'Course I wouldn't be able to get Miri to go with me anyway." Angel gives Miri a poke in the arm. "This girl is happy wearing any old thing."

"I'm the same way," Fen says, pointedly siding with Miri. "I hate shopping. My mom usually has to drag me."

"What about your dad?" Poe is asking. "You said you *used* to live with your mom. Does that mean you live with your dad now? Moved down here to be with him?"

"That's right." Fen nods.

"So late in the school year—odd choice."

Miri glances at Poe. He definitely seems suspicious. Is it just about Miri having a stranger up here, or is it something more? Would Poe know anything about Fen's dad? And who is Fen's dad anyway?

"I got into some trouble in Detroit," Fen is saying, and she blinks over at him—news to her.

"Ooooh, a bad boy!" Angel coos, then winks at Miri. "I always go for the bad boys too, sugar!"

Miri feels her face heating up, but she ignores Angel.

"What kind of trouble?" Poe's eyes are boring into Fen, and Miri wants to shield him, but maybe Fen doesn't need her help. *A bad boy.* Obviously, Miri isn't the only one who's been hiding things.

"Oh, it was nothing, really. I wasn't out partying or anything like that." Fen is watching Miri as he speaks, explaining it to *her.* "My mom caught me after I'd snuck out a couple of times in the middle of the night. I wasn't actually doing anything. I was just . . ." His words trail off, and Miri gets it, thinking of the Detroit/Night soundscapes he's played for her, the guy saying, *The world is jacked.* He snuck out in the middle of the night to record things, that's what it is. But why did he get into so much trouble for that? Wouldn't his mom have understood?

"What did you come up here to borrow anyway?" Poe suddenly shifts gears, and Miri sees Fen isn't quite following.

"A book!" Miri blurts. *"Frankenstein."* What instantly pops into her head. "He needed to borrow it." She jumps up before Poe can stop her, heads to her room, grabs the slim hardcover.

"It's your favorite." Poe intercepts the book as she's handing it to Fen. "You sure you want to give it away?"

"I'm not giving it away," Miri explains. "I'm just letting him borrow it."

"'Beware; for I am fearless, and therefore powerful.'" Poe has the book in his hands, but he hasn't opened it; he's quoting from memory. Miri knows the line. Poe read the whole thing to her when she was little, but then she's read the book many times on her own since then.

"Hey, Fen. Sorry to tell you this way . . . but I just can't . . . it's hard enough . . . looking you in the eye."

It takes a moment for Miri to recognize her own voice.

"But you deserve to know the truth about me . . . about Poe."

It takes another moment for Miri to understand where her own voice is coming from.

"Stop!" She lunges across the table, but Angel scoots back, waggling Fen's phone in the air. "That belongs to Fen! That's private! How did you get that?"

Angel gives a quick shrug. "When I searched him. He didn't even notice."

"Poe has a nickname. The Wizard. It used to be about fixing bikes. Because he was so good at it. But it's not about bikes anymore. It's about—"

"Stop!" Miri lunges again but Angel is too quick.

"The Wizard cooks meth. And he sells it. He's, like, really well known. It's a big operation. And he's dangerous. Not somebody you'd mess with. I'm not sure what he'd do if he found out that I told you, that you were hanging around here."

Miri sits perfectly still this time. "Stop it, Angel. Please!" Trying a different tack. But it doesn't work.

"So I need you to leave me alone. I know you're probably going to want to talk to me about this. But there's no point. I don't want you to get hurt. I don't want you to come back. I want you to stay away from here. Stay away from me."

Finally, it's over. Miri knows it because she spoke it, recorded it. Those were her words. For Fen. Not to be played for anyone else. Especially not Poe. She can't even look at him.

"Why?" Poe's voice is so calm. "Why did you record that?" But he's reaching behind his back—a familiar gesture. The Governor coming out of hiding. "Why did you tell this stranger our secrets?"

FEN

"They're not *our* secrets." Miri has started crying, the tears rolling down her face. "They're *your* secrets." Fen moves to comfort her, but Poe snaps the gun at him.

"Stay where you are," he commands. "I want both of you to stay where you are."

"Or what?" Miri is brushing the tears angrily away. "You'll shoot us?"

Poe jumps up from the table, paces the room, gun in hand. Finally he swings back, zeroing in on Fen.

"I want to know why you have a recording of my daughter on your phone." Eyes blazing.

"And that's not the only one," Angel chimes in, voice sly. "There's a bunch of stuff on here." Thumbing through his files—how'd she even unlock his phone, figure out his password, anyway? "Lots of times he's recorded her talking." Cocking her head at him. "What's that about, hon?"

Miri starts to speak, but Fen puts a hand on her arm. *He's* the one who needs to explain this.

"It's not what you think," he tells Poe.

"What *do* I think?" Poe seems bemused. "I'd like to know."

Fen takes a breath. "I wasn't recording Miri. All those times. I was just recording *sounds*. I make soundscapes. Kind of like . . . a collage of sound."

"'Collage of sound'?" Poe lifts one eyebrow. "What the hell you talking about, kid?"

So Fen explains it all, and Poe seems to relax a little until Fen gets to the part about recording the rooster's crow.

"You'd have to be here mighty early to catch Big Red." Poe's smile turns cold. "Want to explain that?"

"He stayed with me," Miri says, whispering. "What do you care?" Voice growing louder. "I mean, really?" Louder still. "You do all this bad stuff, and you're worried about me sleeping with somebody?"

"You're sleeping with him?" Poe's eyes could burn holes, but Miri doesn't even flinch.

"It's none of your business."

"You live under my roof. I think it is my business."

"I don't want to live under your roof anymore!" Miri is shouting now. "I don't want to be part of your lies!"

Poe sweeps his own chair out of the way, sending it tumbling, skidding across the floor. He moves toward Miri, but Fen stands to block his path.

"Dammit!" Poe immediately turns. "Dammit to hell!" Pacing away from the table and back again, obviously trying to wrest some control. "We're going to sort this out," he says finally, moving close, waving the gun at Fen. "But you! You're not going anywhere!" Glancing over to Miri. "Either of you!" Eyes darting back and forth between them. "I need to go check on Clay, and then we'll have another little chat." Handing the gun over to Angel. "Keep them *both* here until I get back."

MIRI

She wants to go back to her room, take Fen with her, but Angel won't let them out of her sight.

"Clean up the dishes if you want to keep busy," Angel tells them. "But don't get any ideas." Putting on her awful Cockney accent. "I've got the Guv'nor, and I'm not afraid to use 'im."

Would Angel really shoot Fen? Would *Poe* shoot Fen?

Miri doesn't think so, but she's not sure; she's not sure of anything anymore.

Fen and Miri are silent as they clear the table together, but when they get to the kitchen, around the corner from Angel, Miri turns on the water in the sink, hoping the sound will drown out their voices.

"My dad has a whole file on Poe," Fen whispers to her. "He has photos of Clay and Angel, and you."

Miri absorbs this, takes it in.

"Did you know already?" she asks finally. She keeps her eyes down, watching water streaming over the plates. "Is that why you started hanging out with me in the first place?"

"What, you think *I'm* an agent too?" He ducks his head so they're eye to eye. "I'm seventeen. Just a kid, same as you."

"Your dad's an *agent*?" Fully registering this.

"DEA," he says, confirming, and she's almost relieved. It's all out in the open now. Poe will be arrested and she'll go to foster care and Fen will be okay as long as she gets him out of here before Poe gets back.

"Anyway, that's not why I started hanging out with you," Fen is saying. "I had no idea. Dad doesn't talk about his work. And he wasn't home when I got back today. And after I heard your message . . ."

"Sorry about that."

"You could've told me. Before."

"I didn't want you to get hurt. Didn't want this . . ." Nodding toward the living room, where Angel is keeping watch. "I didn't want you involved in my shit."

"I want to be involved in your shit," Fen says. "And it's not *your* shit anyway. It's your dad's. None of this is your fault."

Simple words, but when Fen says them, it's like a weight is starting to lift, a great big rock that's been holding her down.

"We're going to get out of here," Fen says. "We're going to get out of this together."

Miri shifts the tiniest bit, leans what weight is left onto Fen, and it feels so good she wonders why she's never done this before.

"I love you, Miri," Fen whispers, and she nods because she knows it already, and she also knows what she's going to say back.

"I love you, Fen."

CLAY

"Hey, I'm starting to see something," Trent says, just before Clay burps the baby again. He's staring, wide-eyed—at the crystals forming along the bottom.

"Whoa, looking good," Stevie admits, and Clay just nods. He's thinking ahead. How he'll get this batch and give it to Trent and Stevie so that they'll leave. He'll take a little himself, to keep him going. Then he'll make another batch to show Poe, to prove that he's as good as Cora. He doesn't doubt that this stuff will be just as clear, just as pure. Even if he's never done this, he's done it in his mind, Cora teaching him without even knowing.

Maybe he was always going to get here, with or without Poe. So many times he could've gotten rid of Cora's old stash of cold pills buried under the floorboards, never found in the midnight raid so long ago. All the other ingredients are basic—stuff he's always had on hand. Lighter fluid, batteries, Drano. All of it just waiting in the hall closet or under the bathroom sink. Some fertilizer for the garden—and some lye from his aunt when she lived here (she actually made her own soap)—out in the lean-to shed behind the trailer.

Maybe Clay didn't take the time to crush the cold pills so fine like Cora used to do, but everything else is exact. A mason jar with Sharpie lines drawn on it as a measuring cup.

"Magic," Cora used to say. "Abracadabra." After the burping was over, after the liquid had sizzled and clotted its way to crystal. After she had dried stuff that looked something like rock candy by straining it through coffee filters.

Clay doesn't have any coffee filters—he doesn't drink coffee all that much—and he doesn't have any paper towels, either. But he can use an old shirt, one where the cotton has gone thin with age.

He burps the baby again and that's when he hears somebody calling.

"Clay? You in there, son?"

Poe's voice. Not inside Clay's head, but real, and outside the trailer. The bottle goes still in his hand. What day is it? What night? Has he lost track of time? Or has Poe come home early?

"Hey, buddy. I need to talk to you," Poe is saying. "If you could come on outta there, son."

Shit.

Clay should've known this would happen. Poe is always squirrely about going and coming. He should've anticipated Poe returning earlier than planned. What did he do with the handheld anyway? He can't remember.

"Is that the Wizard?" Stevie whispers.

"I thought you said he was gone for a few days, dude!" Trent is whispering too.

"Wondering where you've been." Poe's voice is louder, closer. "Mir says she hasn't seen you much. Everything okay, son?"

"Yeah," Clay calls, looking down at the bottle in his hand. "Yes, sir." The baby needs a burp, and so he twists the cap just a little. The release of gas is just a tiny sound. The smell is stronger. It puffs up into the air, and Clay realizes he didn't grab a bandana or an old shirt to wrap around his nose and mouth, but does it matter? If you're already snorting crank, can the fumes from cooking it do any more damage?

"Clay? I have something to tell you. Some news." Poe's voice getting even louder, closer. He's not on the rickety old front steps—yet.

"Yeah, I was just . . . I'll come out there. Don't come in. The place is a mess."

Clay burps the baby one more time, and then he sets the bottle gently on the kitchen table.

"I'll be right back," he whisper-shouts to Trent and Stevie, whose eyes are showing mostly white like two crazy-scared dogs. "Don't touch it."

"But you have to burp it again, right?" Trent whispers. "You can't just leave it like that."

"I'll be right back." Clay makes eye contact with each of them in turn, so they'll really understand. "Don't touch it. I'll be back in time for the next burp."

And then he is opening the door—just a crack, enough to slip through without giving Poe a chance to see in.

"Hello, sir," Clay says, back to the door. Poe isn't carrying a flashlight. Like Clay, he knows how to walk through the woods at night.

He also knows the smell that's probably clinging to Clay's clothes and skin and hair from the burping.

"I've been kinda sick," Clay says, coughing because his throat really is pretty raw—what happens when you're snorting, even after one day, all acidy back drip. "You might not want to get too close. It might be catching."

There's a long moment of silence, but at least Poe stays put—just outside the ring of porch light. Clay is relieved. He doesn't want to have to look into Poe's X-ray eyes; Clay is certain Poe would be able to see directly into his brain tonight.

"Yeah, you don't look so good," Poe says finally. "You need something, son? Come on back to the house. I made saltimbocca, and there's some left. When was the last time you ate?"

"Nah, I'm not hungry." Clay feels the snot rolling down inside his nostrils—his nose has been running nonstop these last few days and his nasal passages are tender and raw, just like his throat. He tries to sniff the snot back up, but when that doesn't work, he brings his head down to one side, swiping at his shoulder. "I mean, no, sir. Thanks. I'm good. Just getting some rest."

"You didn't check in with me today," Poe says, and his voice is calm, but it's ominous. "Or last night, either. You still got the handheld, right?"

"Oh yeah." Damn. Clay tries to remember where he left it—in the bedroom, maybe? Is this why Poe came back early? "It wasn't working. I meant to try to fix it. But like I said, I haven't been feeling so great."

More silence, then: "You know Miri's been having a friend up here while I've been gone, right?"

Clay looks down at his own boots. "Yeah." Maybe it's better this way, get it out in the open. "But he's a nerd, sir." Still protecting Miri—is that what he's doing? Even after she's been throwing herself at somebody else. "Harmless. Nothing to worry about. The lab's fine."

The lab.

"You been to the lab yet, sir?"

"Nope, not yet. Knew you were keeping an eye on things. The fact is . . . I'm not going to be using the lab much anymore."

Clay takes a couple of steps forward. "What do you mean?" Is Poe retiring? Is he going to hand over his operation to Clay? Is that the news Poe came to tell him? If that's the case, maybe he won't be so mad about what Clay's done, what he's doing right this moment.

"It's a long story," Poe is saying. "I wanted to tell you and Miri, together. But then this kid, this Fen kid, was there."

A surge of anger. "He's a skinny shithead. But I think he's harmless. I'm sorry I didn't keep him away."

Poe waves a hand in the air. "Don't worry about that now. We'll deal with it later. But I do want to get you something to eat. Come on with me, son."

Clay takes another step forward, automatically obeying, but then he remembers. The alien green baby, how it needs to be burped.

"I'll be there in a minute, sir. Just got to change my clothes." Clay turns, puts his hand on the knob, and that's when he hears a burst of whisper-shouting just behind the metal door.

"He said to wait! He said not to touch it!"

"But we need to do something."

"Clay, you got somebody in there?" Moving closer to the porch.

"No, sir," Clay calls back over his shoulder. "I just got to . . ." His hand is on the knob, and that's when it happens: a *WHOMP* like a giant foot stomping down. And the next thing Clay knows, the metal door of the trailer has pinned him hard, his back to the ground. The door weighs a ton and it's red-hot. His fingers make a sizzling sound, but he can't really feel it as he shoves the door off his body. He tries to get up, but there are lights going off inside his head, and there's a heavy ringing in his ears. Finally he makes it to his knees, shaking his head like a dog getting out of a pond, ducking to look behind. Poe is back there, just a shadow lump, starting to move. A voice is yelling something, but Clay can't understand the words.

So he lifts his head, and that's when he sees it. A wall of flame separating him from the trailer—no, that's not right. The wall of flame is part of the trailer; it *is* the trailer.

Screaming voices—coming from beyond the wall of fire— muffled but obviously screaming. Clay stumbles forward and thinks he sees shapes moving inside the wall, inside what used to be the kitchen, fiery shapes, dancing flames. He hesitates but only for a moment. He knows what he has to do. He knows he's the only one who can do it.

You're a god to us, dude.

Clay doesn't like Trent, doesn't like Stevie. But he is a god, right? He is *their* god. And only a god can save them now. Only a god can stop what a god started.

Poe's voice is getting louder behind him, but now Clay is focused on the screaming. He walks forward, straight up the steps—how can the rickety old steps be standing when everything else is gone? Clay takes a deep breath—hot air scalding his lungs—and walks straight into the flames.

MIRI

"Shit!" Fen has grabbed hold of her hand. "That sounded like some kind of . . . explosion."

"Stay here!" Angel races around the corner, waving the Governor in their direction. "Both of you! Stay put!" And then she's gone.

Miri slams off the water in the sink, dashes to the window, looking out, but of course she can't see a thing. The dogs are barking like crazy, though, pulling to the very ends of their chains.

"The house shook." Fen's trying to see out as well. "Did something explode?" Their eyes meet.

"The lab." Her heart starts pounding. Hasn't she heard about meth labs exploding from all the chemicals inside, hasn't Clay told her about that, hasn't she read it in the local paper?

"Where is it?" Fen is asking, but she's already out the door, down the steps, past the dogs barking their heads off.

"This way!" Miri calls back over her shoulder as she crosses the clearing, heads toward the path she never takes. *Off-limits*, Poe always told her. "It's through here!" But she's barely past the trees when another *BOOM* shakes the ground beneath her feet. She stops, centers herself. That didn't come from the lab. It came from . . .

"Clay!"

Miri swings around, crashing headfirst into Fen on the path.

"Wrong way!" she yells, grabbing Fen's hand, tugging him back into the clearing. But when she's on the path to Clay's trailer, she drops his hand. She needs to move faster than Fen can go in the dark. What if Clay's hurt? Shit. SHIT!

"Follow this path!" she yells over her shoulder as she runs. "Just stay on this path!"

Branches are slapping at her face and arms, roots tripping her. One knee even goes down hard on stone, a sharp pain shooting out, but she's up again, moving forward as fast as she can.

"Clay!" she screams at the top of her lungs. "Clay!"

Smoke is tingeing the air, and she can hear a roaring up ahead, can see a brightness through the trees.

"Clay!" she screams again, and she realizes she's not alone anymore. There are other screaming voices up ahead. Angel? Poe? She can't tell. "Clay!"

The air has turned thick, gray puffs drifting through the trees. She starts coughing from the smoke, pulls her T-shirt over her nose and mouth, keeps running.

The roaring is getting louder, and there's a crackling, too, a popping. A few trees up ahead are on fire—leaves bright and burning.

"Clay!" she screams once more, but immediately her voice catches and she's coughing again, much harder than before. She has to lean forward, put her head between her knees. Coughing, retching. The tiny bit of saltimbocca she ate earlier spills to the ground.

When she finally manages to stand up, start forward again, her eyes are blurry, tears gushing, flooding down her cheeks. She swipes the T-shirt along her face, keeps going. She just has to keep going.

"Clay!" She tries it one more time, but her voice is barely a croak. She steps through the burning trees, and that's when she sees it: a wall of fire where Clay's trailer should be.

Clay!

Dark silhouettes are moving against the red-hot wall. Is it Poe? Angel? She can't tell, and she can't get any closer. She's barely inside the clearing, but she's hit a force field of blistering heat she just can't make herself pass through.

Clay!

Something shifts—a flutter of motion. Miri watches—eyes blurred, stinging—as a body emerges from the very center of the fire, walking upright, walking forward. Frantically she swipes at her face, trying to clear her vision. But it doesn't matter, makes no difference at all. The body coming toward her is made entirely of flame.

CLAY

Later he will say he didn't feel any pain.

Later he will say that he saw something dripping down his arm and he tried to wipe it off, but then he realized it was his own skin. Skin dripping, melting away to reveal the white of his bone.

Later he will say he went back in the second time to get Trent, but maybe inside his own head he knows that a part of him went back in for the bottle, as if it would still be intact, not blasted into a thousand bits of melded plastic embedded in skin, trailer wall, a tree ten feet away. As if the glassy chunks inside the bottle would still be waiting in all their crystal glory. As if there were anything left of his creation to save.

MIRI

Hands are grabbing hold of her arms, jerking her backward, dragging her even as she struggles to get away. Is it Fen? No, too big, too rough.

"Get her out of here!"

A bullhorn voice and she's being passed on to somebody else, somebody even stronger—arms made of steel clamped around her.

Let go! Miri tries to scream, but her voice isn't working at all. She kicks at the person holding her, tries to wrench free, but it makes no difference. She might as well be a rag doll carried along under somebody's arm.

Lights are flashing through the trees, zinging off the branches. A flood of people are streaming past her, all of them dressed in black like ninjas, faces covered in alien masks. She hears the piercing wail of a siren—more than one. And then she becomes aware of a *thump, thump, thump* pulsating out over everything.

She looks up as she's being dragged through the woods and glimpses a shiny black body hovering just above the treetops.

Poe's black helicopter. She's seeing it at last.

Miri stops fighting. What's the point? The steel-arm guy carries her to the next clearing and waits while the *thump, thump, thump* gets even louder. No way the helicopter can land—the clearing's not that big. But it does. And then Miri's being pushed inside, strapped in tight—a baby in a car seat.

Fen is suddenly there, on the seat beside her. He's shouting at her and she can make out a few words.

"Walkie-talkie in the truck . . . Dad . . . DEA."

She's so relieved to see him, but the sound inside the black heli-copter is deafening. And Clay . . . She needs to know what's hap-pening with Clay. Desperately she tries to loosen the straps holding her in place, but she can't, so she leans her head as far as she can, pressing her cheek to the glass, trying to see out.

Trees are shooting past—upward, not sideways the way they do when she's riding her bike. Her stomach gives a lurch and her ears pop as the helicopter bumps higher.

At first all she can see is black, but then the fire bursts out of the darkness, turning everything bright for a moment. Miri blinks, trying to find the silhouettes, the body of flame down below. But just then the helicopter banks sharply to the right, and the fire snuffs out.

All that's left to see out the window is the murky, jagged line of Paradise—familiar to Miri even at this height. Another bank to the right, though, and one knob is bleeding into the next, all of them smudging together—a rumpled blanket of dark, impossible to tell one from the other.

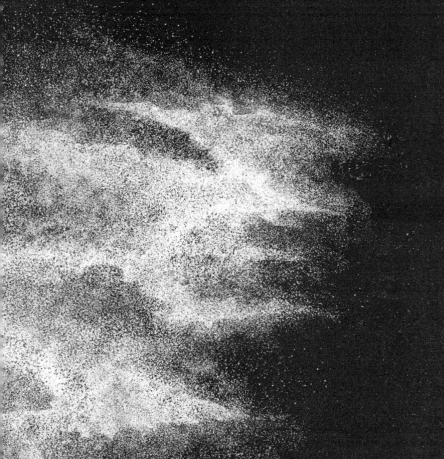

THREE

Deadly Explosion Leads to Drug Bust

LOUISVILLE, KY—A deadly explosion at a mobile home located in a remote region of central Kentucky has left at least two individuals dead and several critically injured.

According to local officials, the cause of the explosion is still under investigation, but the incident led members of a Drug Enforcement Administration special taskforce to a nearby lab in which a large cache of methamphetamine was discovered and seized. Several arrests have been made in connection with what is being called one of the biggest drug busts in the South-Midwest region, but the names of those who were flown to a Louisville hospital to be treated for fire-related burns from the explosion are not being released at this time.

"This is part of a larger, and ongoing, investigation by both the DEA and local police," said DEA Special Agent in Charge Lonnie Kingston. "Releasing names too soon would endanger agents, and possibly obstruct our ability to connect all the dots in this multistate conspiracy to manufacture and traffic sizable quantities of meth."

The Drug Enforcement Administration has headquarters in Washington, DC, but also operates over 200 domestic offices in 23 divisions throughout the United States, along with 90 foreign offices in 69 countries. The objective of the DEA is to bring individuals who violate federal drug laws to justice.

"Drug dealers profit by distributing poison in our communities," Kingston's statement continued. "The DEA continues to aggressively investigate and prosecute all those who seek to benefit from the current drug epidemic affecting so much of our nation."

MIRI

"Where's Clay? Where's Poe? Where's Angel?"

What she kept saying, or trying to say, when they'd first brought her in. Her voice croaking, barely there.

"Where's Clay? Where's Poe? Where's Angel?"

Bright lights rolling above her and faces peering down, including Fen's. A hospital. She was on a stretcher, whooshing along a bright walkway.

"Clay, Poe, Angel."

She'd kept trying to repeat their names, over and over, but nobody seemed to know, and finally her voice had completely given out and she'd let them poke and prod her—a rag doll yet again. And they must've given her something to calm her down, make her sleep. Because she'd started fading in and out—mostly out.

I sleep the sleep of the just.

Some old quote from some old book, she can't remember. And anyway, it's not true, not anymore.

Even with the stuff they keep giving her—or maybe *because* of the stuff they keep giving her—there's fire when she sleeps now. And there's screaming, too. And Clay, always Clay, coming toward her with his flame body, reaching his flame arms out, trying to gather her up.

Special Agent Kingston—Lonnie—doesn't look anything like Fen, so she's not sure she believes him at first. Wispy sandy-colored hair, ruddy complexion, thickened face.

"Where's Fen?" Still croaking, but better. "Is Fen okay? When can I see him?"

And the guy's eyes soften at the name, and that's when she knows. He's the real deal, not some detective or agent or whatever pretending to be Fen's dad to get information out of her.

"Fen's fine. He wasn't exposed to those fumes like you were. He went back to get that walkie-talkie you'd given him from the truck, and was able to call my cell. Lucky thing I'd already had a team prepped to raid Paradise." He pauses. "But it's deadly stuff—what you were breathing in, from the explosion, even for a short while."

Miri absorbs all that, takes a breath—not easy. Her lungs are heavy, like they're full of something she can never seem to cough up.

"Poe," she manages. "Is he . . . ?"

"He's got a lot of burns, but he's going to make it. He's going to be okay."

"Angel?"

A shake of the head, but Miri doesn't pause, doesn't dwell—not yet. She needs to get through the list.

"Clay."

She keeps her eyes open even though she wants to shut them tight.

"He's in ICU. Critical. I'll be honest with you, Miranda, it's touch and go with that young man."

Miranda. Why'd he call her Miranda? That's not her name. But she doesn't bother correcting him. Close enough. He starts in on questions about the others involved in the fire.

"What others?"

Fen's dad checks through the file he's carrying. Photos—isn't that what Fen told her he had? Lots of photos of Poe, of Angel, of Clay; Miri too.

"A Steven Butler and a Trent Witt?" Lonnie looks up. "Friends of Clay's, apparently?"

Miri is the one to shake her head. "Not friends. Assholes. They used to make fun of Clay at school."

"Steven Butler perished in the fire."

Perished. It sounds so peaceful to Miri's ears. What she witnessed at the trailer, what she still sees in her so-called sleep, was and is anything but peaceful.

"Trent Witt is still alive, though like his friend, he's in critical condition."

"They weren't friends." Miri wants it to be clear. "No way."

And Lonnie asks her more questions about that night, the events leading up to the fire, and Miri answers some of them, but her thoughts keep getting tangled up. She keeps snagging on Trent and

Stevie. Buzzards, both of them. They were older, and they weren't in school anymore. But she remembers how mean they were to Clay, how they made fun of him all the time. What would those two assholes be doing anywhere near Clay's trailer?

"I'll come back later, Miranda." He gets up from the chair he's been sitting in. "I can see that you're tired."

Miri reaches out, but she can't grab him because she's in a bed with rails on it, because one arm has a tube attached—fluids and antibiotics, the nurse told her when she asked.

"Fen's dad," she calls before he's out the door. "Agent Kingston." Correcting herself.

He turns, gives her a grin she almost recognizes—another link to Fen.

"Lonnie. You can call me Lonnie," he tells her.

"Am I going to jail?"

Lonnie shakes his head. "You'll be protected. A new life. Don't worry about that right now."

"Foster care? Some kind of foster care?"

"Your dad's alive. He's tough. He'll pull through."

"But he's going to jail, right? I mean, you've got him. He's been caught. He's going to jail."

Lonnie sits down in the chair again, scoots it closer. His eyes are lighter than Fen's, and they're bloodshot, bleary. Deep circles underneath like bruises.

"It should be your dad telling you this, Miranda, but seeing as how he's . . ." Lonnie looks to one side, back again. "Your dad's been working with us. Nearly the whole time. Undercover. Your dad's DEA. Like me."

CLAY

It was that owl he heard, the one Trent pointed out, as they were coming back through the woods.

Your granny saw an owl out her kitchen window, and the next day Pop-pop was lying dead on the floor.

He should've paid attention, he should've known it was a sign. A death owl calling.

Was it his owl? His and Miri's? He hopes not. But probably it was. That's the way things go, at least for him. The baby owl you save from dying turns out to be the one that'll mark your own death.

He wonders if Miri heard it too. He knows she was there, at the trailer. He heard her screaming out. Screaming . . . for him. He saw her—at least the shape of her—standing in the clearing.

But of course hearing the owl was before the fire. When he was walking through the woods with Trent and Stevie. He should've ditched them there in the dark. He should've cut them loose back at the party.

He's sorry that Stevie is dead.

Then again, maybe he's not sorry.

The pain is a living thing eating at you day and night. All teeth and snarl. Like the time he watched inside the early morning woods, watched a coyote eat at a groundhog carcass. He remembers how the coyote just gnawed through the skin and the bones like they were nothing.

The pain gets better when the nurse comes and messes with something in the tube attached to his arm. It gets duller for a little while (the coyote resting before chomping on), but it never really goes away. Coyotes are persistent.

Clay knows what he looks like. At least from glimpsing his arms when the nurses come in to unwrap and rewrap the bandages. He hasn't actually seen his face. They haven't given him a mirror or anything.

But his arms when he catches glimpses are like raw slabs of meat—red and marbled. (Where is the owl tattoo?) He can only imagine what his face looks like.

"We were able to save the nose," he sort of remembers one doctor saying, explaining it to some other doctor. He was in a fog of drugs, so he almost laughed—*Thanks for saving my nose, Doc!*— except that it would hurt too much, even with the drugs. His chest is tight; his lungs feel . . . burned. No other word for it. When he breathes—and he's not even breathing on his own; there's some kind of pump making him breathe—it's like the fire is still going, deep inside his chest.

Clay is a monster. He doesn't need a mirror to see that. He has a nose, but what else is left of his face? He caught sight of Trent after they got the flames out, just before they wrapped him up and carried him away.

Maybe Stevie is better off. Death might've been the better way to go. And maybe it still is.

"He's not out of the woods yet," another doctor was saying just a little while ago, and again Clay just wanted to laugh but he couldn't. He wishes he were in the woods; he wishes he had never left.

FEN

Truth is stranger than fiction.

Isn't that what a teacher told him once? Not in the shit hole but back in Detroit. When he was working on some writing assignment. Truth is stranger than fiction.

Definitely the case here. With Poe.

Fen tries to wrap his head around it—not when he's with Miri. When he's with Miri, all his focus goes to her, making sure she's getting better (she inhaled a shit ton of crap even in the two minutes—or whatever—she was near the fire, so her lungs aren't great), making sure she's not spiraling down into this hole of guilt she's digging for herself about Clay—how she should've been there for him. About Angel, too. (None of it's her fault! He tells her that over and over again.)

When Fen's alone, though, he tries to untangle the whole Poe knot, laying the facts out like he's doing an outline for that Detroit writing teacher.

First of all: Poe is the Wizard—a nickname he initially got because he was good at fixing bikes, but later transferred over because he was good at cooking (not saltimbocca but) meth.

Second of all: The Wizard (the later, meth-cooking one) was actually a cover. "Poe Duke" was really "Special Agent James Poe Duchin," originally with the Cleveland branch of the DEA. (His dad had to run that by him at least three times before he got it.)

Third of all: Fen's dad used to be James/Poe's boss in Cleveland. (Fen's mom knew Miri's mom, and Fen and Miri'd even hung out together on playdates when they were babies—how crazy is that?)

Fourth of all: James/Poe was dirty. He'd taken bribes from drug dealers to look the other way. He hadn't been arrested, but he'd been fired, stripped of his badge, his pension, everything.

Fifth of all: James/Poe wasn't dirty, as it turned out. He'd been framed by his old partner, this dude named Tony something.

Sixth of all (can there be a sixth of all? Actually, yeah there can; it just goes on and on): James/Poe's wife died of cancer—what a truly sucky time for Poe—leaving him with a three-year-old (Miri) to care for on his own. So he left Detroit, just took off. Nobody knew where. Nobody'd heard from him in forever. Fen's dad had tried to locate him because he'd never quite bought the dirty part, but the guy had gone completely off the grid.

And he stayed completely off the grid for a long time.

Until he got back in touch with Fen's dad—backdoor channels. Poe (just Poe now) was living in a remote part of Kentucky, and he'd heard about this crooked agent, who was running things out of the Cincinnati's DEA branch. Of course it was his old partner, the Tony dude, and Poe had come up with a plan to take him down.

"And the plan included cooking meth?" Fen had asked his dad point-blank, that first day he had explained it all.

"It was a way to get to Tony, get into his network. Poe already had a reputation with bikers as the Wizard. We just shifted the business."

"To cooking meth." A statement, not a question. And a *something's wrong with this picture* look that his dad had bypassed.

"Poe was working undercover," his dad had said. "We brought Angel in to help, be his partner."

"So Angel wasn't Poe's girlfriend?" Should he tell Miri that? Maybe not. Would it help or make the guilt worse?

"Angel was undercover too. But you never know what happens when you're working close to somebody."

Okay, not a piece of information Fen needed to know. "So . . . you took all those surveillance photos," he'd said instead. "I saw them on your desk. Poe's place, Angel, Clay . . . Miri. Why'd you do that?"

"All part of the operation, to make everything look real. To make sure everything *looked* real."

"And Angel and Poe cooking meth . . . that was *real*?" Watching his dad closely . . . "And selling meth . . . *real*?" Trying to understand. "And you were okay with it? The DEA was okay with it?"

"Sometimes when you go after big fish . . ." Not meeting Fen's gaze. "You've got to get creative with the bait."

Creative. Fen had let that sit for a minute. *Illegal*—more like.

"Miri didn't know, did she?" he'd asked finally. "I mean, she knew about her dad being the Wizard, but she didn't know about all the undercover stuff, right?"

"Right."

"Wasn't Miri in danger? All that time Poe was . . . doing what he was doing?"

His dad still hadn't looked him in the eye, and he hadn't answered straight off, which *was* the answer right there.

"Well, that just sucks," Fen had told him.

MIRI

When she's finally allowed to see Poe, she's not even sure it's him.
Not until he starts speaking.

"Frankenstein's monster—that's what I must look like." His
voice is still a croak, the way Miri's was before. "Ironic, huh? Your
favorite book."

"'Beware; for I am fearless, and therefore powerful,'" she quotes
back at him, moving closer to the bed.

His body is wrapped almost completely in bandages—no tattoos,
at least none she can see. All that ink—did it melt away in the fire?

Miri starts to cry—silently so he won't hear. (Probably bad to
cry when you see somebody for the first time, when they're so
damaged.)

But Poe's watching her, or at least one eye is. The blue one. The
brown is hidden behind padded gauze.

"I'm sorry, Mir. I'm so damn sorry."

One bandaged hand—more like a paw—rises the tiniest bit off
the bed. She hesitates—will she hurt him if she touches him?

"I never meant for all this to happen." His words come out slow, lots of labored breathing in between.

Miri sits down in the chair, carefully cradles the paw between her hands.

"I never meant to hurt you . . . or Angel . . . or Clay."

The blue eye is filling up, tears spilling over. Miri glances around for something to wipe at the bit of his face she can see, but would that be the wrong thing to do? Would that hurt? Do the tears hurt— saltwater leaking into his wounds?

"Lonnie said he told you everything," Poe continues, and she nods, though it's not exactly true. Lonnie only told her the basics. And then Fen filled her in a little more since his dad has been confiding in him. "What do you want to ask *me*?"

She opens her mouth, but nothing comes out. Where does she start? So many questions. So many lies. Poe has been lying, basically her entire life.

And for what? To get back at somebody, an old partner, who'd double-crossed him years before? Yeah, the guy—Tony, Fen told her his name—was apparently really bad news. And it sounds like they got him. The trip Poe and Angel took—to Cincinnati—it was the final move in a giant chess game, and Poe got his checkmate at last.

Poe was going to tell Miri when he got back—that was his big news—but the whole Fen thing threw him off. He knew Lonnie had a son, he'd known him as a baby, but he didn't expect an older Fen to show up like that, to be involved with his own daughter. For a moment he'd suspected another double cross, but of course that wasn't what was going on.

"Was it worth it?"

Miri didn't even know she was going to ask the question until it was already out. Poe was so desperate to get the bad guy, but didn't he basically become the bad guy himself?

Poe doesn't say anything. Maybe he didn't even hear the question. He's on heavy pain meds, Miri gets it. Third- and fourth-degree burns over 60 percent of his body. Lonnie explained how Poe had tried to save Clay after Clay himself had gone back in to save Trent and Stevie. And then Angel had arrived, and she'd tried to save everybody, which makes Miri's heart ache for this woman she'd so misjudged.

The doctors have said that Poe's healing process is not going to be quick or easy. Skin grafts, constantly warding off infection, scarring. It's going to take months, years. And there will be setbacks, lots of pain.

"No," Poe finally says after Miri isn't even expecting an answer. "It wasn't worth it. I didn't keep you safe, like I'd promised your mom. . . . I put you—everybody—in so much danger." He stops, lets his breathing catch up. "I think I went nuts for a little while. For a long while." Stopping again. "But I promise I'm going to make it up to you. At least I'm going to try."

A nurse bustles in then, tells Miri she has to leave for now, let the patient get some rest.

"I love you, Miri," he says before she gets up from the chair.

"I love you, Dad," she answers. Poe wasn't his first name anyway; time to let that person she never really knew go.

FEN

His mom keeps trying to get him to come back to Detroit. But Fen can't leave Miri. And his dad's on his side, or at least partly on his side.

Fen hears his parents arguing over the phone. He can actually hear his mom's voice from across the room, she's yelling so loud.

"What in the world were you thinking? . . . Why did you agree to let Fen live with you? How could you let him get mixed up in all that? . . . He could've been killed!"

"Thanks, Dad," Fen says after the latest phone call is over, and his dad tells him he can stay "maybe another month."

"Okay, but you got to do your schoolwork," his dad says. "Your mom signed you up at your old school. You have to finish out the school year online."

So that's one (tiny) miracle out of all this . . . tragedy. Fen doesn't have to go back to the shit hole—any shit hole; he can just log in, go online. Homeschool like he always dreamed.

Fen and his dad are living in a Residence Inn in Louisville. Not as permanent as an apartment, not as impermanent as a hotel/motel. And a hell of a lot better than the old Gooch place. There's a pool and a gym and a café in the lobby. And the best part—it's not that far from where Miri is staying. (A foster home situation while Poe's still in the hospital, but not a bad one at all.) Fen walks to her place every day if his dad doesn't have time to drop him off.

Fen's not sure what happened to the "When in Rome" truck. His dad hasn't mentioned it, and it doesn't matter. He never really liked it anyway—not exactly his style. He knows Miri misses her bikes, though; he wonders if she'll get them back when all this is settled—which could take a long while, according to his dad.

"What about the chickens?" Fen had asked Lonnie, thinking about Big Red.

"That old couple on the next knob over took them," Lonnie had said.

"June and Cyrus." Fen had nodded. "What about the dogs? All those pit bulls. You didn't have to . . ." He couldn't finish, thinking back to Miri's gesture—knife to the throat.

"Got a special handler," his dad told him, and Fen was relieved. "They're going into some program just for retraining pit bulls so people can adopt them."

The walk from the Residence Inn to Miri's place is about twenty minutes. Fen always brings his laptop with him so he can play what he'd recorded in the knobs for her—at least what he'd already downloaded. (His old phone disappeared when Angel ran out the door at the sound of the first explosion.) He has a new phone, and sometimes he tries to record things on the street as he goes, but nothing really catches his attention for long. He's surprised how much he misses nature.

On the way to Miri's, Fen keeps passing this one store. Kentucky Gems. It's usually closed, but today it has the open sign in the window, so Fen walks in. New Agey for sure—lots of crystals and healing gemstones. The lady behind the counter looks like an old hippie with her full-length tie-dyed dress and jangly bracelets.

"Just let me know if I can help you find anything, hon," she calls to him.

"Will do!"

Fen idles between the shelves—lots of geodes, some really pricey—broken up in artful ways, polished so the "diamonds" inside really shine. But there are also basic rocks, and in the very back Fen finds a wooden sale bin.

TAKE HOME A PIECE OF KENTUCKY! the sign reads. TWO DOLLARS EACH!

Fen rummages through and finds a few small rocks studded with fossils—shells, tiny sea creatures. He chooses two—both fitting inside his palm—and pulls out his wallet.

"Kentucky is karst country," he tells the hippie lady behind the counter, and she beams at him like he's just won the lottery.

CLAY

He hears the doctors talking about "the other kid," how he didn't make it. He knows that means Trent. So now it's just Clay. A god alone without his subjects.

But that's stupid. Why did he ever think he was some kind of god?

The crank, of course. And that's the one thing this whole shit show brought him: a new understanding of Cora. Why she talked and acted so crazy his whole life. Meth doesn't just make you high, it changes how you think. Meth is like a worm getting inside your brain, wriggling around, making tunnels, holes. Making you think things, see things, that aren't real.

Miri is real. At least he thinks she is. He starts seeing her there by his bed, and then gone again. He's pretty sure she's not a dream or a flashback, because she's not screaming the way she was outside the trailer; she's just talking in a normal voice.

He can't hear the words at first, can barely hear above his own breathing. But gradually, over time, it becomes clearer, what she's saying.

"I'm not going anywhere, Clay. At least not without you. My dad, too. We're going to get through this. Together. We're a family. I'm here, and you're here. And all you've got to do is hold on."

And so he does.

EPILOGUE

The truth is, she misses trees. Now that she's gotten her wish and they've settled in the desert. The stars nearly make up for it, though. Miles and miles of stars—just like she imagined. And the air is dry—good for the lungs, especially damaged lungs, like her dad's, like Clay's.

The assisted-living place they found for Clay is only a couple of miles from Miri's house. She goes there on the new bike she built (the Sportster 2) almost every day after school (not a shit hole).

The physical therapy isn't easy. Clay has to learn how to do things with only a couple of fingers (most simply melted off in the fire); he has to learn to walk with no toes (all gone). He still has some trouble breathing, and talking. He gets things mixed up inside his head, and he'll say the wrong word for something basic like a chair. He insists the pain's not so bad—though it probably is, according to the doctors.

Fen had to move back to Detroit with his mom, but he and Miri text constantly, FaceTime for hours at night. (She can't believe how she ever lived without a cell phone.) Fen sends her soundscapes— amazing mixes of the stuff he recorded in the knobs. Miri plays them for Clay sometimes, and she knows the familiar chirping and droning and babbling of brooks make him happy even though he continues to refer to Fen as "Bambi" and sometimes "skinny shithead."

Miri's dad is fixing bikes again, custom building a few for select clients. He pulled through all the skin grafts without too many complications. He's scarred basically everywhere, no tattoos—mostly melted away like Miri'd imagined under those bandages. But it doesn't matter; he's alive.

And he's back to his real (cleared) name: James Duchin. The DEA reinstated him, offered him a consultant job, but he told them no.

"Too much time wasted already," he said.

Technically, Miri is Miranda Duchin—the name Lonnie knew her by when she was a baby back in Cleveland.

"Miranda's from *The Tempest*," her dad told her once they got that sorted out. "It was your mom's favorite play."

"Old-lady name." Clay's take. "You're not an old lady." So it never stuck.

Miri rides the Sportster 2 to school, but on weekends she's focused on the new bike she and her dad just built together. A sand dragger like she kept talking about back in Kentucky. Light and low, built for speed, but with a vintage dirt bike's knobby wheels to dig in when they need to.

Miri doesn't want to race, even though there *are* a few desert races not that far from where she lives, definitely regulated, not fly-by-night like the old days. But she still wants to learn how to ride on sand—not sure why exactly, except that it's not like any other surface. Sand's totally unpredictable, constantly shifting.

"When you pull away," her dad is instructing her now—first time they've got the new bike out in the middle of nowhere, desert sand everywhere—"remember to keep the motor revving, much higher than usual, at least to start. You've got to dig yourself out of the hole you're creating with your bike. And then you've got to stay on top of the sand. Remember to keep shifting—fast, clean. Get sloppy and you'll literally get sunk again."

At first Miri thinks her dad is overexplaining—mansplaining, isn't that what it's called? But it turns out he knows a thing or two. It takes a million tries. The knobby wheels keep lurching, chomping at the sand; the gears won't shift quick enough, and the high rev makes everything too fast to control anyway.

She's just about to stop for a while, take a break, when the front wheel spins out of its crater and the back wheel doesn't catch and snag. All at once the bike—she's nicknamed it the Angel—is gliding over the gritty surface, sailing like a boat on water. She hears her dad whooping it up behind her, but she keeps her eyes straight ahead—squiggly heat lines far off on the horizon.

Everything goes smooth, weightless, and she holds on to the feeling as long as she can. A few more feet, a few more minutes, and she knows the sand will probably trap the wheels, suck the bike back down. But that's okay. Miri doesn't mind sinking, not as long as she knows how to pull herself back up.

Author's Note

I love Shakespeare. Always have. Probably because my dad quoted from Shakespeare plays like *The Tempest* throughout my childhood. My dad was an actor, and started his own theatre in Kentucky called Pioneer Playhouse.

Lots of plays, including *The Tempest*, found their way into my novel *Here's How I See It—Here's How It Is*, a story about a young girl growing up in a theatre much like Pioneer Playhouse. From that book on, *The Tempest* was like a seed—planted, taking root, sprouting. Over time I became fixated on how I could use the iconic story of a father and daughter stranded on a deserted island as framework for something new.

At the start of *The Tempest*, we learn that Prospero and his daughter, Miranda, were shipwrecked long ago, the consequence of some double cross in Prospero's mysterious past. Ultimately, *The Tempest* is about revenge. But it's also about first love, sacrifice, betrayal, and rebirth.

At first, I thought about going futuristic with my retelling. Possibly postapocalyptic. It worked with the whole deserted island thing. But I'm a Kentucky writer—all my books have been set in Kentucky—so I decided to place my story in a world I know.

The knobs are real, though in my fictional story, I take liberties and rename landmarks. In my story, the magic practiced by Prospero is linked to something real—something darker, more menacing.

The opioid crisis has been devastating in Kentucky. Friends, sons and daughters of friends—so many lives lost to addiction, to overdose. No family is immune anymore.

Wrecked isn't a retelling of *The Tempest*; Shakespeare's play was more of a jumping-off point for me. As I write a book, I listen carefully to what my characters have to say, and Prospero's daughter—at least the one inside my head—was definitely ready to be heard.

Acknowledgments

Thank you . . .

To Caitlyn Dlouhy, who sometimes makes me laugh, sometimes makes me cry, but always makes me write harder. Thank you from the deepest of deeps.

To Jane Lazarre, who first told me I had a voice and something to say. To Joanna Cotler, who has taught me so much about books and art and life. To friends near and far who listen and inspire and keep me sane: Jennifer Daniel, Anna Benlow, Susan Hill Long, Zoé Strecker, Fe Myers, Tricia Murphy, Kimberly Neuhaus, Julia Langham, Julie McAllister, Alison Craig, Laura Jack, Sheryl Byfield, Kathy Ault, Malissa McAlister, Amanda Manning, Rebecca MacNeal, Callie Minks, Catherine Thomsen, and Florence Hinds. To LouAnn Kruse, and her late husband, David Reber, who've long provided space to work—really couldn't have finished this one without a room of my own. To my mother, Charlotte Henson, who gave me a love of reading and so much more. To my father, the late, great Eben Henson, who truly believed we are such stuff as dreams are made on. To the kick-ass team at Caitlyn Dlouhy Books—Michael McCartney, Clare McGlade, Tatyana Rosalia, and

Alison Velea—who created a killer cover and a truly gorgeous book. To Justin Chanda, Jon Anderson, Michelle Leo, Chrissy Noh, Anne Zafian, and all the dedicated folks at Atheneum Books for Young Readers and Simon & Schuster, who work so hard to bring books into the world.

And finally, to my children, Daniel, Lila, and Theo (and Sara too!), and (again) to my husband, Tim, who are, quite simply, everything.

Books Used by the Author Directly or as Inspiration

Frankenstein, by Mary Shelley. Dover Publication edition, 1994.

How to Survive the End of the World as We Know It: Tactics, Techniques, and Technologies for Uncertain Times, by James Wesley Rawles. Published by Penguin, 2009.

Methland: The Death and Life of an American Small Town, by Nick Reding. Published by Bloomsbury, 2010.

The Tempest, by William Shakespeare. Published in the First Folio, 1623.

Zen and the Art of Motorcycle Maintenance: An Inquiry into Values, by Robert M. Pirsig. Published by William Morrow Paperbacks, 2005.